FIVE REASONS WHY YOU'LL LOVE THIS BOOK . . .

When Holly becomes **ELECTRIGIRL**, the words become pictures! Look out for the awesome comic strips throughout!

"Holly's brother Joe is my favorite. The artwork of the comic sections is phenomenal!"
JACK, AGE 10

"I couldn't stop reading — it felt as if I was part of the adventure. Full of suspense and mystery from start to finish."
LENA, AGE 9

Shockingly good! For an electrifying, hair-raising adventure, look no further!

Holly's earlier adventures can be found in **ELECTRIGIRL** and **ELECTRIGIRL AND THE DEADLY SWARM**

FOR ELIZABETH MOULFORD,
IN MEMORY OF HER
CLEVER STARDUST DADDY, BILL
— J. C.

FOR MY SISTER, THE BEST EVER
SUPERHERO MENTOR
— C. B.

Electrigirl and the Invisible Thieves is published by
Stone Arch Books, A Capstone Imprint
1710 Roe Crest Drive
North Mankato, Minnesota 56003
www.mycapstone.com

Text copyright © Jo Cotterill
Illustrations copyright © Cathy Brett

Electrigirl and the Invisible Thieves was originally published in English in 2016.
This translation is published by arrangement with Oxford University Press.

Library of Congress Cataloging-in-Publication Data is available on the
Library of Congress website.

ISBN: 978-1-4965-5670-7 (Library Binding)
ISBN: 978-1-4965-5669-1 (Paperback)
ISBN: 978-1-4965-5673-8 (eBook pdf)

Summary: The only thing Electrigirl didn't have was the perfect superhero outfit.
Now she does, and nothing can stop her.

Designer: Mackenzie Lopez

Printed and bound in Canada.
010407F17

ELECTRIGIRL
AND THE
INVISIBLE THIEVES

By Jo Cotterill   Illustrated by Cathy Brett

STONE ARCH BOOKS
a capstone imprint

Hello, super-cool readers!

I'm so thrilled that Cathy and I are bringing you a THIRD story in the ELECTRIGIRL series! This time we've introduced new characters who have their own superpowers, and it's one I know loads of you would love to have: invisibility!

I love reading comics and graphic novels, and my favorite of late has been the amazing story EL DEAFO by Cece Bell about a girl who loses her hearing and has to wear a really big hearing aid. She just wants to fit in and have good friends, but other stuff keeps getting in the way. It's totally brilliant and clever and the artwork is awesome, so do check it out!

Since the last ELECTRIGIRL book was published, I've been out and about visiting lots of schools and talking all things superhero and electrical! If you'd like me to visit YOUR school, just visit my website at jocotterill.com to find out how!

Happy reading! And if something goes missing, it might be an invisible thief!

CHARACTER PROFILES

HOLLY is not your average 12-year-old. A lightning strike gave her a scar and electrical powers, turning her into **ELECTRIGIRL**!

JOE is Holly's superhero-obsessed brother. Her self-appointed mentor, Joe likes planning and telling Holly what to do!

IMOGEN is Holly's best friend, and their many differences complement each other well. Clever and talented, Imogen loves drawing and solving puzzles.

LIN is an agent of a top secret organization. She speaks seven languages, is a black belt in karate, and flies a helicopter.

PROFESSOR MACAVITY is super-evil, super-smart, and Holly's nemesis. Always working in the shadows, when will she strike next?

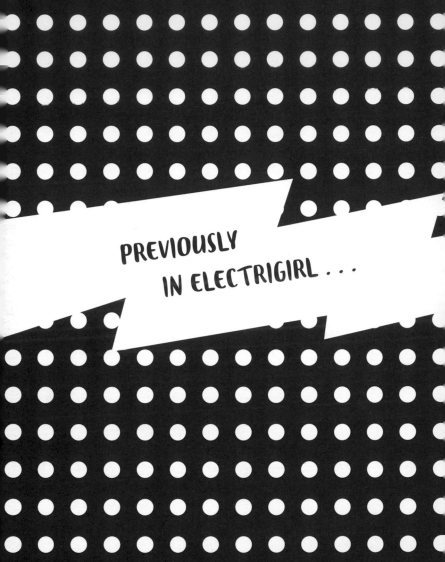

PREVIOUSLY
IN ELECTRIGIRL . . .

CHAPTER 1

The Bluehaven Gazette

CRIME WAVE HITS BLUEHAVEN

Items such as pens, paperclips, candy, and small toys have all been reported missing from a range of shops along the boardwalk, prompting some Bluehaven businesses to declare that the town is in the grip of a crime wave. Detective Claire Roberts from the Bluehaven police told the *Gazette*: "The nature of the thefts suggests children may be responsible. We would like to make it clear that stealing is stealing, no matter what the age of the thief or the value of the item stolen, and we take this kind of thing very seriously indeed." Anyone with information is invited to call the number at the bottom of the page in complete confidence.

It was a hot day at the end of summer break, and my best friend Imogen, my brother Joe, and I were down in the town, hanging out together. We'd stopped at a small store to see what we could buy with the precious little allowance money we had left. As usual I'd forgotten my money entirely, so couldn't buy anything anyway. Instead I'd been idly scanning the newspaper headlines.

I nudged Imogen and held out the *Bluehaven Gazette*. "Have you seen this?"

She read it. "Wow. Hardly anything ever gets stolen in Bluehaven. But now kids may be stealing candy!"

"It'd be so easy to do," I said. "I mean, it's summer, and this town is packed. Anyone could slip something in their pocket. I'm surprised the shops have even noticed. Hey, Joe! Have you seen this?"

My brother was standing next to a rack of postcards, examining the watch on his wrist. Except it wasn't really a watch. About a week ago, Joe had received a package in the mail, and inside it was the best present he'd EVER received (and I mean EVER, and that includes the year he got a full-size Lego Batcave for his birthday). It was a real spy gadget, befitting the mentor of a superhero (me, **ELECTRIGIRL**, obvs). It had come from Steve, head of a mysterious government agency I sort of worked for. I was a bit disappointed that Joe got sent this amazing techy thing instead of me. But then Joe started talking me through the fifty-seven menu screens and I nearly fell asleep it was so boring! I'm just not a gadgety sort of person. I like the running around parts of being a superhero. My brother can be the tech-wiz! Plus, to be honest, I don't have a good track record with electronic items and safety — they tend to blow up or melt . . .

"Joe," I said again, holding up the newspaper. "This. Have you seen it?"

Joe came over. "I think I've just set the alarm," he said. "We'll know in a minute." He paused. "Or I might have told it to compute the exact distance to Jupiter. It's a bit confusing." He took the paper from me. "Ha! Fantastic! Bluehaven's answer to real crime. Hang on — hold the paper for me." He lifted his watch and pressed a button on the side. There was a faint click. "I THINK I just took a photo," he said.

I carefully refolded the paper and put it back on the stand. The shopkeeper glared at me.

"Time to go," I said quietly to Imogen. "I'm getting a mean stare."

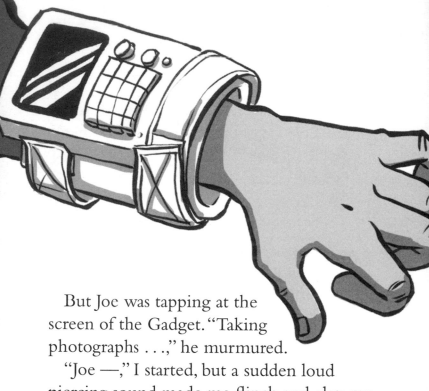

But Joe was tapping at the screen of the Gadget. "Taking photographs . . .," he murmured.

"Joe —," I started, but a sudden loud piercing sound made me flinch and clap my hands over my ears. My powers, activated by possible danger, sprang to the surface . . .

WHEEEEEEE!

CHAPTER 2

As Joe said it, I felt my powers drain away. There was no danger now. Becoming electrified wasn't a good thing all the time — a scar pattern appeared on my chest and arms, and I had a tendency to give people electric shocks if they got too close! "Find out who the thieves are?" I repeated.

"What a good idea!" exclaimed Imogen. "We can do some true sleuthing, like by researching. And for once, it's got nothing to do with **Professor Macavity**."

My brother nodded. "It's the perfect job for **ELECTRIGIRL**."

We smiled at each other. All three of us had nearly died at various times, thanks to **Macavity**, and we were in no hurry to meet her again! The last time we'd seen her was in Cornwall, and to my relief, there'd been no sign of her since.

"We could hunt for thieves right now," said Imogen. "Only I really want to go to the library first."

I laughed. Imogen was the best friend any superhero could have, but even hunting bad guys couldn't distract her from her favorite hobby for long. "Another art book?" I guessed.

Imogen smiled. "Is that OK? I reserved one. I just need to pick it up; then we'll snoop around."

"Of course." I linked arms with her. "Joe, we're going to the library. You can come as long as your Gadget isn't going to make that awful noise again."

"Mmm." My brother was tapping through menus again, but he kept following behind.

Bluehaven library was hardly more than a big room. The librarian, Mrs. Vankowicz, had been there twenty years and knew Imogen very well. Mrs. Vankowicz had an American accent and a mind like a steel trap, as my dad would say. She knew every single book in the library and could remember what you had checked out three years ago. "I know what you've come in for," she said with a smile. "Reservation, right?"

"That's right," said Imogen.

Mrs. Vankowicz looked along the shelf. "Clump . . . Clump . . . oh. That's odd. It's not here. Hang on a minute." She called to another woman who was putting books back on shelves. "Fran, have you seen that lovely big art book Imogen Clump reserved?"

Fran frowned. She was helping out at the library over the summer and you didn't want to get into a conversation with her because you'd never get away. Last time I'd been here, I'd heard all about her bad knees and her water retention and her allergy to guinea pigs. She talked like every sentence was a question. "Sorry, Glenda, I haven't? It might be in the back room?"

"I'll just go and have a look," Mrs. Vankowicz told Imogen with a smile. "Just a minute."

While Imogen was waiting, I wandered over to the children's section, which was hardly more than a corner. I liked books but I found it hard to concentrate long enough to finish one. If I had to sit still for any length of time, my legs went all jiggly and I really wanted to go and run around outside. My math teacher, Miss Howlett, called me a fidget.

There was a computer in between the shelves that no one was using. I sat on the swivel chair in front of it and spun around. Mrs. Vankowicz was taking aaaa-ges finding Imogen's art book.

"You're looking nice and tan?" Fran observed to me.

OH NO! She was trying to talk to me! Should I pretend I hadn't heard?

"Been on vacation?" Fran asked. Then she sighed. "I haven't been on vacation for years; I'm agoraphobic, you know? Can't step outside my house without getting the jitters; the library is one of the few places I feel safe? The doctor said it can be triggered by a traumatic incident, and I think it was because . . ."

Desperately, I looked around, but there was no help. Joe was sitting on a beanbag chair, his eyes glued to the Gadget screen. Imogen was at the counter waiting for Mrs. Vankowicz to return. There was no one else in the library at all. Perhaps if I didn't look at Fran, she might realize I wasn't interested.

Above the shelves were the displays. There was the summer reading challenge, where kids could sign up to read a number of books over summer break. There were the posters about toddler groups every Tuesday and Thursday. There was the . . .

OH.

OH WHAT . . .

My hands clenched on the arms of the chair as I stared up at the wall.

Professor Macavity's face stared back at me.

"But I said high ground's no good, not with my asthma . . .," Fran prattled on.

AND THAT'S WHEN I BLEW UP THE LIBRARY.

CHAPTER 3

I was halfway to the door when my powers drained out of me like water down a drain. My legs turned to jelly and I reached out to grab a nearby bookcase to stop myself from falling. Imogen was at my side instantly. "Are you OK?"

"Fran!" Mrs. Vankowicz pulled her assistant to her feet. "Fran, can you hear me? We need to get out of the building!"

Joe strode past me, giving me a black look.

Out in the parking lot, poor Fran collapsed in hysterics, wailing and stuttering. "You should slap her face," Joe said helpfully.

"Joe!" I said, horrified.

"That's what they do in movies," he explained.

"I think we should call an ambulance," Mrs. Vankowicz said. "And the fire department." She pulled out her cell phone. Fran continued to wail and clutch at her hair.

Joe glared at me. Then he sat down next to Fran and started talking to her in a soothing voice. "It's all right. You're going to be all right. It was just a malfunction, that's all. Everything will be all right . . ."

I stared at him. Joe watched a lot of superhero movies, and quite often there was a woman screaming. Maybe he'd learned how you were supposed to talk to them?

I could tell Imogen badly wanted to ask me what had happened, but we couldn't have a conversation here — there were too many people around. Some passersby stopped to help, and within a few minutes, the emergency services had arrived. The paramedic insisted on checking me over, but apart from a scratch on my hand from a bit of glass, I was completely unhurt. "What's this on your forehead?" she asked curiously, placing a finger on my head.

"Oh . . ." Self-consciously I rearranged my bangs to cover my scar, left over from my first encounter with **Professor Macavity**. The scars that appeared when I was using my powers always disappeared afterward — except for the one on my forehead, which looked like a kind of fern or thin tree branches. I didn't really like people asking about it. After all, I couldn't exactly explain how I got it. "It's just a scar," I said.

"Goodness," said the paramedic, "I've never seen one like that before."

I shrugged. "Am I OK? Can I go now?"

"Yep." She smiled at me. "Lucky escape, huh?"

You have no idea, I thought to myself. "Joe, Imogen, you coming?"

Mrs. Vankowicz was pale but controlled. "You kids go ahead," she told us. "The library will be closed for some time while they make sure it's safe. Imogen, I'm afraid I left your book in there."

"Don't worry, Mrs. Vankowicz," said Imogen. She looked upset. "I'm so sorry."

"Goodness, dear, it wasn't your fault. I'm just glad you're all OK."

As we headed away from the library, I heard the paramedic say in a puzzled voice, "That's funny. Where's my stethoscope? I'm sure I put it down right here . . ."

Some kid giggled. I frowned, staring at the sidewalk. I hadn't found anything to laugh at.

"What happened in there?" Joe asked me in a low voice.

I didn't know how to answer. I hadn't lost control like that since the very early days of getting my powers. "Did you see the poster?" I asked instead. "The one about **Professor Macavity** running for mayor here?"

Imogen flinched at the mention of the name and Joe stared at me, mouth open. "Mayor?" he repeated in disbelief. "**MAYOR**?"

"I guess Mr. Foley's stepping down," I said. "Maybe his wig has had enough of being photographed." Everyone knew Mr. Foley wore a wig, but Imogen and Joe didn't seem to realize I'd made a joke.

"But — she can't," said Imogen, shaking her head. "She's a wanted criminal! You can't have wanted criminals running for mayor."

"I don't know how it's happening," I said, "but I'll bet Steve doesn't know."

Joe huffed. "Well, he flipping should. Hang on, I'll send a message."

We ducked into an alleyway and waited until it was clear. Joe tapped the screen on his wrist and held it up in front of his face. "Video message," he said clearly. The Gadget did nothing. "Video message," he said again, more loudly. There was no response. Joe cursed under his breath.

"Joe!" I said, scandalized.

"Oh, just give me a break. I'll remember how to do it in a second." He tapped a few more buttons and then suddenly the Gadget went **PING**! and an electronic voice said "Begin Message." Joe went, "HA!" and then remembered it was recording. "Oh, sorry. This is a message for Big Boss from Thunderbolt."

"Thunderbolt?" I mouthed at Imogen. Joe ignored me.

"**Macavity** is here. In Bluehaven. Running for mayor. Holly — or — **ELECTRIGIRL** — saw a poster. Please advise."

He pressed another button and the Gadget said, "Sending video message."

We waited. And waited.

After a minute, I said again, "Thunderbolt?" and tried not to giggle.

"I was allowed to choose my own codename," Joe said, offended. "I like it. Anyway, we've got a bigger problem than **Macavity**, haven't we?"

"What?"

Imogen was astonished. "*You*, Holly."

"All that training!" Joe planted his feet apart and glared at me. "You shouldn't lose control like that. What happened back there?"

I hesitated. In my mind I played back the events in the library. I was sitting calmly on the chair . . . I saw the poster . . . and then **WHAM**! Powers everywhere! There was no warning, no control . . . I felt my face redden. I didn't know what had happened. I could make balls of electricity. I could send shockwaves down steel cables to cause tremors deep underground. I could even create an electrical pulse that could knock humans unconscious. And yet I'd just gone berserk in a perfectly safe library! It was so embarrassing.

It must have been a glitch. I just needed to do some more training. Get back on top of things. The poster had taken me by surprise, that was all. I'd calm down, go back to basics, focus on my breathing like I did at the beginning. I'd be OK.

All of this passed through my head in a matter of moments. I looked at my brother and best friend and I just couldn't admit what had really happened. Instead I shrugged. "Maybe there was a short circuit somewhere in the library's electrical system. I was a bit sparky, but it wasn't me — really."

Joe frowned. "It *wasn't* you?"

"Are you *sure*?" asked Imogen.

I put on a hurt expression. "Do you think I would lie about something as important as this?" Behind my back I crossed my fingers.

Imogen's face cleared. "Sorry, Holly." She gave me a hug. "Of course we don't think you're lying."

Joe's Gadget suddenly beeped and the small screen lit up. MESSAGE RECEIVED. WILL INVESTIGATE. STAND BY FOR FURTHER INSTRUCTIONS.

"Nothing we can do right now then," Joe said, sounding disappointed.

"Let's go up to Holly's hillside," Imogen suggested. "They might have opened it up again." The hillside above the town was my favorite place in the world and was also where I had been given my powers. The **CyberSky** phone tower, partly responsible, was being dismantled, and the area had been under quarantine for a few weeks.

"Good idea," agreed Joe. "Holly could get in some practice up there too."

I trailed along behind them, trying to look enthusiastic. But in my head, all I could hear was my own voice . . .

You lied to them.

You lied . . .

CHAPTER 4

I'D NEVER LIED TO IMOGEN BEFORE. Joe, yeah, loads of times — I mean, everyone lies to their own brother, *don't they*? I probably lied to him four or five times a day, on average: stuff like, "I never heard you calling me," or, "there aren't any cookies left," etc. But Imogen — no. I didn't need to lie to Imogen because she was my friend and she was always totally on my side (except when her brain was being warped by evil cell phones, but that's another story).

I trudged along behind Imogen and Joe, trying to convince myself that it was only a little lie, and that it wouldn't matter anyway because I would make absolutely sure it didn't happen again.

We took a little footpath through the houses that led up a steep flight of steps to the coastal path. I loved living by the sea, and as we climbed higher, my spirits began to lift too. So when Imogen next turned around to glance at me, I was able to give her a real smile. Fingers crossed we'd be able to get up to my hillside too. I felt a bit weird about the **⊛CyberSky** phone tower being taken down. I wondered if we would ever find out how it had transferred superpowers to me.

We rounded a corner — and there, in front of us, was a tall metal fence blocking our way. A sign on it said:

DO NOT CROSS: CONSTRUCTION WORK. HARD HATS MUST BE WORN AT ALL TIMES. NO ENTRY TO THE PUBLIC.

"Oh," I said, disappointed. "They haven't finished. But the tower isn't there any more."

Imogen peered through the metal links. Beyond was a scattering of trees and a wide expanse of grass leading to the cliff edge. "I can't see any people, or diggers, or anything. Maybe the workers forgot to take the fence down when they finished."

I felt frustrated — and rebellious. I missed my hillside. "We can go around it," I said, pointing to where the fence ended to our left, the post standing in a concrete block.

"We're not allowed," said Joe.

"There's no harm in taking a look," I argued. "I'll just go beyond the trees so that I can see the spot where the tower was. If there's no one there, we'll know they just left the fence behind by mistake." Even as I was talking, I was walking to the end of the fence and slipping around it.

Imogen gasped. "Holly!"

Joe sounded stern. "Holly, you're going to be in MEGA-trouble."

"I'm just going to LOOK," I snapped. "Honestly, what kind of trouble could I be in? I'm **ELECTRIGIRL**, for goodness' sake."

I turned away from them and took three steps toward the little patch of trees — and then I heard Imogen **SCREAM** as a monstrous white figure, too big to be human, loomed out from behind the trees and stretched out thick white arms toward me.

MY POWERS LEAPT TO THE SURFACE . . .

My powers stopped instantly and I felt suddenly sick and dizzy. "Quarantined?" I repeated stupidly. I stumbled back around the fence, my stomach threatening to do something nasty with my last meal.

"Holly, are you OK?" asked Imogen.

"Is SHE OK?" exploded Joe. "Are WE OK, is more like it! Do we LOOK like a threat, Holly? I mean, seriously — what were you THINKING, blasting us like that? Good thing the fence deflected most of it, or we could be TOAST!"

I stared at him in horror. "Are you — I didn't realize . . ."

"Yes we're FINE, no thanks to you," he went on angrily. "Lethal weapon, that's what you are — never forget it. We're starting training RIGHT NOW."

Lin came around the side of the fence, pulling off her gloves and producing something small and metallic and cylindrical from a pocket. "Oh . . .," I said, feeling incredibly stupid. "I'm really sorry about this, Lin. I've never seen anyone in one of those . . . suits . . . up close. I was only — ow!" Lin had pressed the metallic cylinder to my finger and it had shot a tiny needle into it. A drop of blood welled from my fingertip. "Ow . . .," I said again, sucking my finger. "What did you do that for?"

Lin didn't answer. She was staring at the side of the cylinder. Then she nodded briskly and put the cylinder away. "You're clean," she said. "Wrong DNA."

I stared at her, my finger still in my mouth. There was so much to ask and say that suddenly I couldn't speak at all. It was Joe who stepped forward and said, holding out his hand, "Good to see you again, Lin. What's going on?"

To my astonishment, Lin shook my brother's hand in a professional manner. I was instantly jealous. Lin was my total hero, and yet all I ever seemed to do in front of her was look like an idiot. She nodded to Imogen too, and completely ignored me.

"Contamination from the phone tower," she said. "When the contractors took it down, they dropped that gray ball from the top of it — remember it?"

I certainly did. It was the gray ball into which the lightning had crashed, and the gray ball that had sent the arc of green electricity smashing into my chest, giving me my powers.

"Turns out the gray ball wasn't empty," continued Lin. "It was full of green liquid. The ball cracked, and the liquid seeped into the ground. We've had to bring in a bio-hazard unit to deal with it."

"What is it?" asked Joe.

"Some kind of organic-synthetic mixture," Lin said. "We're not entirely sure what it is, but it seems to react with certain types of human DNA. You remember that the **CyberSky** cell phones had a strange effect on some people? We think maybe it was dependent on their DNA."

I glanced at Joe and Imogen, who were gazing at Lin with rapt attention. "Oh yeah, DNA," I said carelessly. "That would explain it."

Everyone looked at me. "You don't know what DNA is, do you, Holly?" asked Joe.

"Of course I do!" I retorted. "It's in your blood. It's . . . stuff that makes you who you are."

Joe narrowed his eyes. "*Stuff*?"

"Yeah, stuff. In your . . . blood . . ." I crossed my arms over my chest and then uncrossed them again. "Everyone knows that."

"DNA," said Lin in her cool voice, "stands for DeoxyriboNucleic Acid, which is a molecule that carries genetic instructions. Every cell in your body carries this molecule and your DNA is particular to you — every person's DNA is different, which is how we are all able to be very slightly different in our eye color, height, the speed we can run, the shape of our bones, our mental ability . . . everything."

"Hmm. It seems to have skipped the mental ability part in your case, Holly," observed my brother.

"Hey!" I said. "How do YOU even know this stuff?"

"Duh," said Joe. "Every evil scientist tries to mess around with DNA. It's in practically every comic ever written."

I turned to Lin, trying not to actually look at her face because I still felt stupid. "So why is my DNA wrong?"

"In order for the green liquid to have an effect on the human body," Lin said, "your DNA needs to carry a particular sequence of genes. Yours doesn't."

"Oh," I said.

I had absolutely no idea what she had just said, but Imogen asked quietly, "What about *my* DNA?"

Lin looked at her, but before she could say anything, the Gadget on Joe's wrist beeped and projected a holographic message into the air:

AGENT DISPATCHED TO YOUR LOCATION

"Well, that's a bit late to the party," I said. "Lin's already here."

Lin made a kind of snort. "I wasn't here for *you*. Did you call for assistance?"

"Sort of," I said, wondering if I would ever, EVER say something that wasn't completely dumb in front of Lin.

"How do they know where we are?" asked Imogen.

Joe shook his wrist. "The Gadget has built-in GPS." He glanced at me. "Global Positioning System."

"I know what that is," I snapped, only slightly fibbing. I did know the letters, though not what they stood for.

A faint thrumming noise reached our ears, growing louder by the second. "That sounds like . . .," murmured Imogen.

"Motorbike!" I said, suddenly feeling a LOT happier. Because there was only one person we knew who rode a motorbike, and he was **MEGA-COOL**.

"Oh no . . .," I heard Lin mutter, with a sigh. "Not *him* as well."

The next moment the bike came charging up the coastal path behind us, ignoring all the signs that said you couldn't do that, and the wheels skidded to a halt.

The rider, clad all in black, removed his helmet and grinned at us. "So," said Maverick cheerfully, "the gang's all back together again!"

CHAPTER 5

"Mav!" I exclaimed joyfully. Maverick was another super-cool agent like Lin, but unlike Lin, he was super-friendly too. He was addicted to caffeine and drank way too much coffee, but he was always up for an adventure. For some reason Steve thought Mav was a bit of a pain, but Imogen, Joe, and I all thought he was **BRILLIANT**.

"Doing all right, Lin?" called Maverick, running his hand through his spiky hair, which made no difference at all.

Lin rolled her eyes and turned away, pulling her gloves back on.

Mav grinned. "I love you too!" he called. Lin pretended she hadn't heard. "So," said Mav, hanging his shiny bike helmet on the handlebar, "you guys wanna know what's going on in Supervillain-World?"

"You mean in the world of **Macavity**?" Joe asked eagerly. "Yeah!"

"Come this way." Mav turned and headed off down the coastal path, away from the fence. I cast a look back at Lin, but she was already suited-up and walking back to the hillside — my hillside — where the ground was saturated with weird green goo.

"What about your bike?" Imogen called after Mav. "You can't just leave it here; it might get a parking ticket."

"Or stolen," added Joe.

Mav said nothing but held a key over his shoulder and pressed a button. The bike went **BEEP BEEP** and then vanished.

Joe, Imogen, and I stopped in our tracks. "WHOA," said Joe.

"Oh . . . my . . . gosh," said Imogen slowly.

I, as usual, could think of nothing to say because the inside of my head was going WHAT THE HOW DID WHY THE BIKE GONE JUST VANISHED HOW, etc.

Mav always carried incredible types of technology with him. He had once hypnotized a whole bunch of people with a tiny neural tranquilizer.

"Cloaking device," breathed Joe in a low whisper. He reached out a hand toward the air and felt around. "It's still there. I can feel it. But I can't see it."

"Light refraction," said Imogen. "But I didn't know it was a real thing."

"Are you all coming or what?" shouted Mav. We hurried after him.

The coastal path wound up around the back of the houses in this direction. In fact it wasn't even really "coastal" because you couldn't actually see the sea from this section. It was the section of the path most people didn't bother with because the view was terrible.

Maverick stopped when we were on an open piece of ground and turned to check. "Good," he said, satisfied. "We'll see anyone coming before they hear us. So — fill me in."

Joe told him about the poster in the library.

"She can't run for mayor," I said. "She's a criminal."

"Weeeeeeeeeell," said Mav, making the word five times longer than usual, "yes, she is, but technically . . . she isn't."

"Technically?" I repeated blankly. "What do you mean, *technically*?"

"Well, under the law," said Mav, "she isn't. I mean, you and I know that she kidnapped Imogen and tried to use her brain, and she tried to make hundreds of people jump off a cliff, but the thing is . . . there's no proof."

"But everyone knows she's insane!" I cried.

Mav shook his head. "We've done a lot of work clearing up after her and making sure nobody actually remembers what happened. So you see, nobody knows what she did. And you can't be arrested for being insane. It's not a crime."

I glared at him. "You're the government. You should be able to do something."

"I know what this is about," interrupted Joe. "This is corruption."

"What?" I said.

"Corruption." Joe nodded. "It's like the Gotham police force before Commissioner Gordon took over. It was full of people being bribed so that the Joker could get away with murder."

"**WE'RE NOT IN A COMIC**, Joe," I said sarcastically.

"It's the same thing," he insisted. "Happens everywhere. Everywhere people have money and power — and **Macavity** has both."

I turned to Maverick. "It can't be that, can it? Tell me she's not buying her way out of this."

He looked uncomfortable. "Hey, it's nothing to do with me. I just follow orders. Steve said we can't touch her yet. She's got a really fearsome legal team. And friends in high places."

I shook my head. "I don't believe this. So you're telling me that she could walk along this path here, and there would be nothing you could do? We'd have to let her walk on past? Seriously?"

"I know how you feel," Mav told me with a sympathetic look, "but that's the way the world is. We have to find another way."

"We could just push her off a cliff ourselves," muttered Imogen. I reached to squeeze her hand. Imogen had practically been turned into a zombie thanks to a phone from **CyberSky**, the company owned by **Macavity**. Not to mention nearly losing her brain in **Macavity's** Machine, which was trying to take over the internet.

"Then I'd have to arrest you for murder," Mav told her sternly. "Don't even think about it, kids. We're not vigilantes."

"All great superheroes are vigilantes," declared Joe.

"There must be something you can do," I told Maverick fiercely. "You must have access to classified information …" My limited knowledge ran out. I burst out in frustration, "Who *are* you anyway? What *is* your department?"

Maverick looked surprised. "Didn't Steve tell you?"

"No!"

"Oh." He seemed genuinely taken aback. "Well, I dunno why he wouldn't tell you. You are working for us, after all. Maybe he just forgot to mention it. We don't actually use the name very often, since for all intents and purposes we don't exist."

"What name?" I asked through gritted teeth. Mav could be infuriating!

"Paranormal Operations," Mav replied. "It's a big department. I work in one branch of it — the branch you work for too. It's called Weird Experiments and Rogue Science."

There was a pause while we all processed this. Then Joe said, "Paranormal Operations: Weird Experiments and Rogue Science? **POWERS**? *You work for a department called* **POWERS**?"

"Yeah," said Maverick. He grinned. "Cool, isn't it?"

CHAPTER 6

If I'd thought Joe was annoying since he got his wrist Gadget, he was super-annoying now that he'd found out we were working for a department called **POWERS**. All that evening and the following morning, he kept trying to talk to me about it — so much so that Mom was in serious danger of overhearing. "Joe," I hissed at him finally, "shut up!"

Of course, *that* was the bit Mom overheard. "Holly!" she said sharply. "Don't talk to your brother like that. You know I don't like you using that phrase; it's rude."

"Sorry," I muttered, shooting Joe an angry glare. He stuck out his tongue at me.

"Do you two need something to do?" Mom asked. She pushed a hand through her hair. Her other wrist was still in a cast from an accident she'd had while we were on vacation in

Cornwall. It had sort of been my fault, and I felt guilty whenever I saw the cast. She'd also come very close to discovering my secret identity, but luckily Steve had smoothed over all of that. I was, however, under strict instructions to "stay away from drama." Which was kind of difficult to do when you had thousands of volts at your fingertips.

"It's just that Nicky's coming over," Mom went on, "to discuss the carnival. I've promised to help out with the Bluehaven preschool float, since they've had a couple of people drop out at the last minute. So thoughtless, when people do that. The preschool depends so much on fundraising, and this year they're doing a beautiful under-the-sea theme. All the toddlers will be dressed up as starfish and shrimps." Mom's eyes went slightly misty. "I can't sew, of course, with this wrist out of action, but I'm going to help with painting — and I expect I'll be riding on the float too, helping out with the children. It would be very nice if you two would come and help too."

Joe and I exchanged horrified looks. Helping out on a preschool carnival float? **NO WAY**! Suddenly he was my best ally again.

"Oh . . . uh," I said.

"We'd love to," Joe lied, "but I've signed up for a race at school next term, and Holly's promised to help me train."

I nodded so hard that my head ached.

Mom looked disappointed. "Oh, I see. Well, stop bickering then and get out from under my feet. And Joe — can you do something about that new watch of yours? It keeps beeping in the night and waking me up. If it keeps doing that, I'll be ringing up that shop you ordered it from and asking for a refund."

"Oh — yeah." Joe looked panicked for a moment. "Don't worry, I'll turn all the sounds off."

We ran up to his room, shut the door behind us, and breathed sighs of relief. "We can't let Mom think we need occupying," I said. "Especially not if Nicky's around."

Nicky was Mom's best friend, and the two of them were always getting involved in "good causes." If it had the word "campaign," Mom and Nicky would be there, doing whatever the campaign asked them to. They'd protested against Macavity's **CyberSky** building when it opened in Bluehaven, because they were concerned about the radiation from the cell phone tower on the hill. If only Mom knew what was REALLY inside that tower!

On second thought, it was better she didn't know. She'd probably pack us all up and move to a deserted island in the middle of the North Sea or something. "I wonder how long they'll take to decontaminate the hillside," I said, to no one in particular.

Joe wasn't listening. He was fiddling with the Gadget again. "There's a whole menu here for scanning," he said in surprise. "Jeez, I wish I'd known. I could have scanned the library for electrical faults."

I felt my face redden.

"Or I could have scanned Fran for any injuries," Joe went on. "Though probably not in front of the paramedic."

"No," I agreed. "She might have asked where you got the Gadget. Or wanted to borrow it since her stethoscope disappeared." I glanced out of the window and pondered idly. "Maybe someone stole it when she wasn't looking. One of the thieves in Bluehaven's crime wave. We haven't really started trying to track them down, have we?"

"Holly, I don't think anyone would steal a stethoscope in broad daylight," Joe scoffed. "Everyone was far too worried."

"Not the person who giggled," I pointed out. "You know, the kid? Who giggled. They weren't worried."

He stared at me. "There weren't any kids outside the library except for us. And none of us giggled."

"What?" I frowned, puzzled. "Then where did it come from? Someone definitely giggled, I heard it." A sudden wave of dizziness came over me, and I leaned forward, holding my head. "Ooh."

"What's the matter?" Joe asked.

"I feel a bit . . . sick."

He jumped up in alarm. "Don't be sick in my room! Go to the bathroom!"

I sank sideways onto his bed. "No, it's OK . . . I think it's passing . . ."

"Don't you dare puke on my Avengers comforter!" Joe instructed.

"Thanks for your concern . . .," I said faintly. The comforter felt cool against my cheek, and in a few moments the sick and dizzy feeling passed. I sat up, gingerly. "Ooh. Yuck. That was weird."

"Maybe you had a bad cornflake this morning," Joe said. "That reminds me — we need to restart your training. You OK now?"

"Yes, I think so."

"Good. Where should we go?"

We both thought about this. The hillside was my favorite place to practice, but that was out of bounds thanks to the green goo contamination. I had sometimes practiced in the backyard, but if Mom and Nicky were going to be chatting in the kitchen, that was a no-go. I couldn't risk either of them glancing out of the window and seeing me using my powers!

"I know," said Joe. "We'll go back to the dump."

Bluehaven Recycling Center was where I had done most of my early training, back when I still didn't have full control over my powers. It was full of discarded electrical items — perfect for me to practice on!

We headed out of the door just as Mom's friend Nicky arrived. "Hi, Nicky, bye, Nicky!" I said breathlessly.

Nicky, her blond hair escaping from her ponytail as usual, looked a bit surprised. "Oh!" she said. "You off somewhere nice?"

"The beach!" yelled Joe as we jogged down the hill away from the house.

I giggled. "Can you imagine what she'd say if we told her we were going to the dump?"

We stopped to get Imogen along the way. Her mom was on the phone when we got there and just waved at us, pushing some money at Imogen and mouthing, "Buy ice cream."

"Thanks, Mom!" said Imogen.

"Ice cream," I said, suddenly feeling VERY much in the mood for mint chocolate chip.

"Later," said Joe. "Training first."

I pouted. "My powers work MUCH better after ice cream."

"No, they don't," he said sternly. "That's an enormous pants-on-fire lie."

I felt a bit tired by the time we got to the recycling center. Maybe I hadn't slept very well last night? Come to think of it, I didn't remember waking up, but . . . maybe it had been the wrong sort of sleep, where you don't get refreshed?

Joe checked the site to make sure there was no one else around. The Gadget on his wrist **BEEPED**. Joe pressed a button and the Gadget said in an electronic voice, "Weather today:

Bluehaven. Temperature: seventy-three degrees. Wind: easterly."

"Wow," I said sarcastically. "That's *really* helpful to know."

Joe fiddled with it. "Why doesn't this thing have a simple "mute" function? Mom's going to go nuts if I can't stop it from talking."

He pressed another button and suddenly a thin blue beam came out of the side of the Gadget, swept all the way around us in a 360 degree arc, and then proclaimed: "Three humans within 400 meter radius."

"YES!" Joe punched his fist into the air. "Finally, something useful! Awesome!" He saw us staring at him and said, "What? This is **AMAZING**. The Gadget can tell us when there's someone approaching. We're the only three people here, which means we're clear to do your training."

I nodded, impressed despite myself. "That is kind of helpful."

Imogen said, "Are you guys OK if I do some drawing? I mean, there's not much I can do while you're zapping stuff, is there?"

"You go ahead," I told her. "Just don't sit near anything electrical."

"All right," said Joe to me. "Let's go back to basics. This is all about breathing and control. Switching things on and off, and steady, targeted energy pulses. OK?"

"OK," I said. I yawned and my brother frowned.

"I hope you're taking this seriously, Holly. Your powers are too strong not to be controlled."

"Yes, yes," I said, annoyed. I rubbed my hand over my eyes. "Let's get on with it."

Joe stood back.

I CLOSED MY EYES AND FOCUSED. MY FINGERS TINGLED . . .

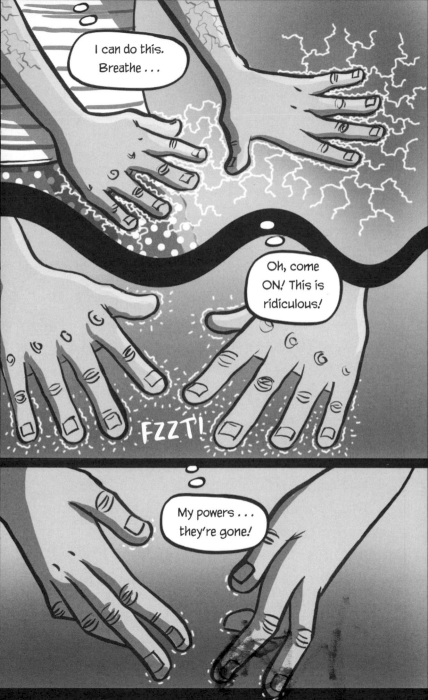

I blinked. What just happened? I rubbed my hands, but there was nothing there . . . no electricity . . . nothing.

A cold wave of fear washed over me. Where were my powers?

WHERE WERE MY POWERS?

Joe strode over, frowning. "What's the matter?"

"I don't know," I said. "I just . . . they're gone. I can't do anything."

"Holly," Joe said, sounding irritated, "they can't just GO; you're not trying hard enough."

"I am!" I cried. "I don't know what's wrong! I do the breathing, I focus, but they're gone!"

Joe shook his head. "You're out of practice, that's what it is. We haven't done any training since Cornwall. You've forgotten how to do it."

"Oh, get off my case," I snapped. "You don't know what you're talking about. Are you me? NO. So stop telling me what's wrong."

My brother looked furious. "*I* don't know what I'm talking about? How dare you! I know more about this stuff than you EVER have! You just bumble around blowing things up, and I'm the one who's put all the effort in to keeping you safe!"

"SAFE!" I yelled. "Don't make me laugh! Who was it who decided he was going to jump off a CLIFF in Cornwall and needed ME to save his life? HUH?"

Joe's mouth fell open and he took a step back. He looked shocked. "I was poisoned, you know that," he mumbled. "I can't believe you'd blame me for that." Then the fire was back in his eyes. "You know your problem, Holly? You're *grumpy* and *rude*, that's what you are. You don't want to train? **FINE**. But don't waste my time." He gave me one last glare and then turned and ran out of the recycling center. Within a few seconds, he was gone.

I stared after him, hardly able to believe what had just happened. Was he walking out on me? Was my mentor resigning?

I jumped at a sudden hand on my arm. I'd almost forgotten that Imogen was there. "Hey," she said gently. "You OK?"

The sympathy in her voice made my eyes fill with tears. I sniffed. "I don't know what's happening to me, Imogen," I said miserably. "My powers . . . I think . . . I think they might be leaving me. I don't think I'm **ELECTRIGIRL** any more."

CHAPTER 7

Imogen decided that what I needed right then was ice cream, so the two of us walked down the road into Bluehaven and onto the boardwalk. It was bustling with people, and we had to weave our way in and out of the crowds. I hated being hemmed in. "Can we go somewhere quieter?" I muttered to Imogen as we waited in line at the ice cream kiosk.

"Sure," she said. "Let's take our ice cream down to the beach."

The tide was out, so we could walk near the rocks at the end of the sandy beach. Beyond them were rock pools and coves, and although there was a scattering of people there, we found a place where we could sit down in peace.

I licked the ice cream from the sides of the cone and stared at the sea. I felt very tired still, and a bit queasy — but I told myself that was because it had been a long time since breakfast, and I was just hungry.

Imogen sat beside me and said nothing, which I was grateful for. I didn't know what to say, and I didn't want to be asked questions. One of the best things about Imogen was that she always seemed to know exactly how I was feeling, and she knew that I just needed quiet company until I was ready to talk.

I finished my cone and licked my fingers. Then I sighed.

"Do you know what's wrong?" Imogen asked, which was a very sensible question.

"No," I said. "It's like . . . you know when a car engine doesn't start right? It sort of stutters. It feels like that, with my powers. Like they're stuttering, not running smoothly. I turn the key, and nothing happens, or it happens all at once."

Imogen nodded slowly. "Do you think you should talk to someone about it?"

"Like who?" I asked, though I knew who she was going to suggest.

"Well — Steve," she said, proving me right. "I mean, maybe he can help."

I bit my lip. "I dunno. I keep remembering what Joe said when all this started: that I shouldn't tell anyone because doctors would want to operate on me and dissect my brain, and stuff like that."

"But this is *Steve*," Imogen said. "He's on our side. And he knows stuff — more than we do. He probably knows about superpowers and things like that. Whether they go . . . on and off, or something."

I nodded. "I suppose. I just . . . I feel kind of embarrassed, you know? And a little sick. Maybe I'm just coming down with something. What if everything's back to normal tomorrow? I'd feel really stupid bothering Steve for nothing."

"Want to see something?" Imogen said, changing the subject. She put her sketchbook on her lap and opened it up. "I've been designing."

I took the book from her and my eyebrows practically climbed into my hair. Imogen had been designing **ELECTRIGIRL** costumes! "Oh wow!" There were five different variations, all of me in various poses, with different costumes.

"I'm not sure if you should have a cape or not," Imogen said. "I mean, they're really superheroey, but not very practical. What if it got caught on a door handle or something?"

"These aren't *tights*, are they?" I peered suspiciously at one design.

She grinned. "I know how you feel about tights! They're leggings. And all the designs have a mask, of course, to hide your scar and to make it harder for people to recognize you."

I gazed at the drawings. "Imogen, these are really cool. You're so talented."

"Oh . . . well." She waved a hand, as if batting the compliment away, but she looked pleased. "I thought I would send them to Steve and the department could see if they could make one of them for you. I can draw but I can't sew. But I bet they've got someone at **POWERS** who can."

I gave a little laugh. "I still can't believe it's called that. Do you think they did it on purpose? Decided which name would be really cool and then just made up words that would fit the letters?"

"No," said Imogen, "because it really fits, doesn't it? I mean, weird experiments and rogue science is kind of **Macavity** entirely isn't it? Using science to create robots and poisons and green goo that somehow affects people with a certain kind of DNA . . . if that isn't weird, I don't know what is."

I was feeling better by the minute. "You're so great," I said, giving Imogen a hug. "I'm so glad you're my friend."

She went pink. "Oh. I'm glad you're my friend too."

I got to my feet and brushed sand off my shorts. "Want to go and watch the rides?"

She beamed. "Best idea ever." She put her hand down behind her to push herself up but withdrew it immediately, exclaiming, "Ew!"

"What is it?"

She held out her hand to me. It was dripping in some kind of green liquid. "Someone must have spilled something here," she said, her nose wrinkling in disgust. "There's a big puddle of it. Oh — no, look. It's not been spilled. It's seeping out of the rock wall there, see ..." Her voice trailed off as we both stared at the wall, from which a thin trickle of green oozed. Our gazes traveled up the wall, up over the rocks, the layers of history mapped out, up to the line against the sky ...

"That's my hillside up there," I said, and my voice croaked. "Where the *CyberSky* tower was. Where the ground got contaminated ..."

"By the toxic stuff that alters people's brains . . .," whispered Imogen. "If they have the right DNA . . ." She gave a sudden jerk and flapped her hand. "Oh no, get it off, get it off, **GET IT OFF**!"

"Imogen, it's OK." I tried to reach out to her, but she was panicking like crazy, squeaking, and crying, and hitting her hand on the rocks, trying to wipe the green stuff off.

"There's a rock pool," I said, pointing.

She ran over, slipping and sliding on the rocks, and plunged her hand into the water, rubbing it over and over with her other hand. "What will it do to me?" she said, and her breath came in short gasps.

I put my arm around her shoulders. "Nothing. I bet it won't do anything at all. It's not like it's in a phone. Or struck by lightning."

"But Lin said . . ." Imogen gulped. "She said it had an effect on people with a certain type of DNA. You KNOW what the phones did to me. I went like a zombie — I didn't remember who I was or who my friends were. So I already have the right kind of DNA. What if . . . what if this green stuff is now in my body, changing it? What if I wake up tomorrow and . . . and . . . I'm *evil*?"

"That could never happen," I reassured her. "It just couldn't. You're Imogen. You're my best friend. And if . . . if something does happen, then we'll fix it, OK? Like we always do."

She looked at me with wide, frightened eyes. "You promise?"

"I promise," I said, giving her a big hug. "I will *always*, ALWAYS rescue you. Because you're my best friend."

She tried to smile. "Thanks, Holly. It's probably fine. I only got it on me for a few moments. I just feel a bit shaky."

"I know what you need," I told her seriously. "Cotton candy. Lots of it. In a big pink, fluffy cloud."

She smiled. "Is that a medical thing?"

"Yes," I said. "Doctor Holly prescribes cotton candy. Sugar for shock."

"We haven't actually had any lunch," Imogen commented.

I shook my head. "Cotton candy provides all the nutrition a traumatized person needs."

She laughed. "We'd better go and get some then."

We climbed down off the rocks, but I glanced back. "We need to tell **POWERS** about the green goo. And we should probably do something to stop other people from getting near it."

"My sketchbook!" exclaimed Imogen. Ten minutes later, the rocks were covered in our paper notices bearing the words:

DIAPER EXPLOSION, STAY AWAY

and

MY BABY SISTER POOPED ON THIS ROCK. AVOID UNTIL HIGH TIDE.

There had been a lot of giggling as we wrote them.

Imogen stood back and looked at our work. "I need a new sketchbook, since we've used up all my spare pages."

"We'll buy one on the way to getting cotton candy," I said. "In fact, *I* will buy you a new sketchbook." Then I felt in my pockets. "Or . . . I will *owe* you a new sketchbook."

Imogen rolled her eyes. "You never have any money, Holly. Come on."

It was early afternoon, and the beach was absolutely packed with people, many of them walking all the way out to the water's edge.

"Tourists," said Imogen, with a sigh, skirting the edge of a group of excited kids who had found a dead jellyfish on the beach. I shuddered and felt a lurch in my stomach. Definitely coming down with something.

As we reached the boardwalk, I saw a familiar figure. "Joe!" I shouted.

He turned, and when he saw it was me, he looked kind of guilty and pleased and embarrassed all at once. "Um . . . sorry about earlier," he said.

"What?" In the panic over Imogen's hand-in-goo incident, I'd completely forgotten our argument. "Oh, that's OK. Listen, we need you to contact Steve." I told him about the leaking green stuff on the rocks.

I'll say one thing for my brother, he catches on quick. Within seconds of my beginning to tell him the story, he was videoing me with the Gadget, and sending it to **POWERS.** Almost immediately an answer beeped on his wrist: **RECEIVED. WILL SEND TEAM.**

"Team," I said, impressed. "Wow."

"You covered the rocks in paper, right?" asked Joe. "So they'll be able to spot the right place."

"Yes. Paper from this." Imogen showed him what was left of her sketchbook. "We're on our way to buy a new one."

Joe glanced at the pages and then grabbed the book from her. "You drew these costumes for Holly? Awesome!"

"Shhh," I said, looking around to make sure no one was listening. But to be honest, I could have shouted "I AM A SUPERHERO!" and no one would have taken any notice apart from giving me annoyed stares. Bluehaven was that kind of place.

Joe was scanning the designs with the Gadget. "Oh," said Imogen, blushing, "they're not finished or anything . . ."

"They're great," Joe told her. "I'm sending them to **POWERS**. Holly needs a costume. If she ever gets back to training, that is." He gave me a pointed look.

"All right, all right," I said. "Later, all right? We've got a schedule. Sketchbook buying, cotton candy eating, carnival ride watching."

"I'll come with you," Joe said. "I'm trying all the options on the scanning menu."

"You're the most fun ever," I said sarcastically. "Let's go."

All the main street shops are on the road behind the boardwalk because on the seafront, all anyone wants is cafés and beach shops and ice cream trucks. So we headed away from the crowds and down a side street called The Snicket, which always makes me laugh because it sounds like something rude you do with your nose. Overhead the unmistakable droning of a helicopter filled the air. "Coast Guard," I commented.

"Not this time," Joe said. "That's **POWERS**."

I looked up. Between the rooftops I could see a sleek black chopper gliding through the sky toward the sea. "Are you sure?"

He nodded. "It's the same one we saw in Cornwall."

I sighed. Last time we saw that helicopter, it was being flown by Lin. She was so cool.

The stationery shop was practically empty of customers. Imogen took a long time choosing a sketchbook (even though they all looked the same to me) so I wandered over to a table in the middle of the shop. It was covered in the latest craze — tiny erasers in the shape of cakes, animals, toys, landmarks, fruit . . . They were kind of cute, but I couldn't imagine why anyone would want to collect them. How many erasers could you actually need? And no one would ever use a tiny pink doughnut to rub anything out, since it would spoil the look of the eraser. So you might just as well make them out of plastic — except no one would buy them then.

I picked up a couple, marveling at the detail. And then I saw the prices, and I hastily put them back again.

"Have you seen these?" I called to Joe in a low voice.

He cast a glance at the table, unimpressed. "Girl stuff," he commented. "You girls are obsessed with collecting pointless things."

I was about to retort that he was a fine one to talk with his collection of superhero figures and sticker albums, when a familiar giggle caught my ear, and suddenly, right in front of my eyes, the tiny pink rubber doughnut jumped off the table and disappeared into thin air!

My jaw fell open. **WHAT HAD JUST HAPPENED?**

CHAPTER 8

I tugged at Joe's sleeve, keeping my eyes on the table of erasers. "Joe," I strained. "*Joe* . . ."

"Holly, I'm really not interested in rubber pineapples."

"No, look . . . !"

He turned — as a miniature ice cream cone and a strawberry lifted off the table and vanished, just as the doughnut had done.

"What the . . . ?" murmured Joe.

"Is it . . . magic?" I whispered. I couldn't quite believe I was asking the question. *Magic?* It wasn't real — was it?

Joe snorted, and the sound must have carried, because all of a sudden there was a mini landslide of erasers on the far side of the table. And then a very faint shimmer in the air, and the woman over by the door said, "**HEY**!" as her bag fell off her shoulder all by itself.

"Not magic," said Joe. "*Invisibility*. We've got an invisible thief! Get him, Holly!"

Before I knew it, I was running out of the shop, looking wildly from left to right as I reached the street, my brain spinning. An *invisible* thief? Someone was *invisible*? But — that was as impossible as magic!

More to the point, how did you follow an invisible thief?

There were people strolling along the sidewalks, and to the right of me, nothing seemed odd. But to the left, someone turned around and looked puzzled, and a woman's dress wafted to one side as though in a breeze, and so I set off that way. It was hard to know how fast the thief was going. Once I caught sight of that slight shimmer in the air again, but then I lost it. Then as I reached the bakery, I lost *all* my clues. There were no disconcerted pedestrians; no shimmering air; no people tripping over invisible objects. Heart thumping, I walked to the end of the street, looking around. Nothing.

To be honest, it wasn't really all that surprising. I mean, they could stand still and I'd just walk by them . . .

"You lost them?" Joe came panting up to me.

I shrugged, annoyed. "They were *invisible*."

Imogen, clutching a brand-new sketchbook, hurried over. "I thought you might get bored waiting for me! Did I take too long choosing my sketchbook?"

"I lost the invisible thief," I said.

Her mouth dropped open. "What?"

Joe suddenly hit himself on the head. "**OH**! I'm so stupid!"

"Tell me something I don't know," I said.

Joe was fiddling with the Gadget. "I should be scanning the area! Using infrared!"

"What even is that?" I asked.

Joe held up his arm and moved around in a slow circle. The screen on his wrist showed a read-out of glowing red and yellow lights.

"Infrared is the detection of heat," he said. "So even if someone's invisible, they're still producing heat — and the Gadget should be able to detect them."

"So that thing can see people even when they're invisible?" I asked.

"Yup."

"Wow."

He paused. "Nope. No weird readings. They must have left."

Imogen finally broke in. "Will someone please tell me what's going on?"

Joe and I explained about the disappearing erasers in the shop. "I wonder at which point they disappear?" Joe mused. "I'm guessing the thief's clothes are also invisible, so there must be a kind of force field around them. Anything that gets close to their body is swallowed up by that field."

I ignored him because he was doing that techno-science-babble thing that doesn't require anyone else to participate. "How can someone be invisible?" Imogen was asking me.

"I dunno," I said. "But then how can someone have electrical powers? I mean, it's all a bit crazy. And it explains the crime wave thing, and why no one has caught the thief yet. You could steal *anything* if you were invisible."

She stared at me, eyes so wide I could see the whites of them.

"What?" I asked nervously.

"You don't think . . ." She swallowed. "You don't think it's because of that green stuff, do you? I mean . . . what if someone fell in it, and it made them invisible?" She lifted up her hand and stared at it hard. "Is my hand . . . oh Holly, is my *hand* going to disappear?"

I took hold of her hand and waggled it around. "It's fine, Imogen. You're totally getting paranoid about this. We'll ask **POWERS** to look at it, OK?"

She took a breath and nodded. "Maybe they could look at *both* of us?" I knew she was referring to my erratic powers.

"Oh, I'll be fine. I feel better already," I said cheerily. "We still haven't had any cotton candy. And I want to watch the rides. Come on." I set off along the boardwalk, suddenly desperate to get moving again.

"I wonder where the invisible thief is now?" muttered Joe.

"Don't care," I said — and then I stopped, because right up ahead was a sight that chilled me to the bone in the hot sun.

Professor Macavity — my evil nemesis, the woman who'd tried to kill me and my friends more than once — was on the boardwalk.

SPARKS GATHERED AT MY FINGERTIPS . . .

As my power vanished like a soap bubble popping, I could do nothing but watch the **Professor** walk away.

"Aargh!" Frustrated, I kicked the wall of the boardwalk. "*Ow!*" Now I was angry AND in pain.

"Thank goodness you didn't zap her in full view of everyone!" Imogen gasped.

"I tried," I said through gritted teeth. "But it didn't work."

"And a good thing too," snapped Joe. "What did you think you were doing, confronting her like that in public? Are you insane?"

"Oh, shut up," I snapped back. "I want my cotton candy. In fact I need two of them now."

"Then you can bring your own money next time," I heard Joe mutter.

"I'll buy it," Imogen said softly. "Don't worry, Holly. Let's try to put it behind us. Come and watch the rides, ok?"

I felt awful: guilty and angry and sick and frightened and hot and cold all at once. *Why* weren't my powers working? Was I really losing them?

How could I go back to being ordinary Holly again?

CHAPTER 9

We bought cotton candy and headed over to the carnival that arrives in March every year and stays until October. They have a helter-skelter and a waltzer and a carousel and a couple of those tiny rides for children that have a fire engine and a train and a bus that just go round and round for three minutes.

Imogen stopped as we reached the helter-skelter and grabbed a strand of cotton candy from her hair. "I'm watching from here today." She didn't say anything more about **Professor Macavity**, I noticed.

"I'm off to the other side," said Joe, and left. *Also* not saying anything about **Macavity**.

I stuffed a large bite of cotton candy into my mouth and headed for my favorite watching place.

I don't know when Imogen and I started watching the rides. I think it must have been a couple of years back when we ran out of money one day (it happens a lot when you buy ice cream and cotton candy). Mom wouldn't give us any more, so while she sat and read a book, Imogen and I stood and watched the rides wistfully. Within a few minutes, we'd realized that watching the rides was almost better than watching TV, and now it was one of our favorite things to do. Even Joe enjoyed it.

You see, "watching the rides" wasn't just watching. It was a whole game in itself, with rules that we'd invented over the years. The winner was the one with the most points after an agreed length of time (or when we were forced to go home). You got one point for any of the following things:

- A child crying because they'd dropped their ice cream
- A person with REALLY bad sunburn, like lobster-red sunburn
- Parents trying to drag their children away from the rides
- People asking unnecessary questions, when

all the information is right in front of them on signs
- A seagull stealing food
- A teenage boy with his underwear showing at the top of his pants

You got five points for any of the following:
- Parents lying to their children about not having any money left (and then saying, "let's go and buy a snack")
- Someone budging in line
- Fairground injury, e.g. scraped knee, friction burn from the slide, split lip from the carousel, bumped head on mini-roundabout child ride
- Two people kissing on the Ferris wheel
- A child letting go of a balloon

You got ten points for:
- Emergency shutdown of ride
- Parent losing a child (who usually turned up almost immediately)
- Finding money of any kind on the ground
- Someone's wig blowing off while they were on a ride
- A hot air balloon
- A granny race on the bumper cars (this had

actually happened once and it was so brilliant and so funny that Imogen and I agreed it should totally go on the list, even though it had never happened again since)

You kept count in your own head, and it was a strict rule that you couldn't cheat. You had a better chance of winning if you kept moving around the edge, so you could see as many people and rides as possible. My favorite place to watch was by the carousel, which was an old-fashioned one with three rows of horses bobbing up and down, and an organ in the middle with mirrors and flashing lights.

I was still angry and confused and now I was sticky from the cotton candy too. But keeping count in my head had a calming effect, and before long I felt much better. I'd got up to twelve points in my head when a family walked past and I overheard the dad say to the mom: "I think she'd be good for the town. We need more business here." I just *knew* he was talking about **Professor Macavity.**

– OR MAYBE NOT!
ZZZZZT!
FZZZ!
SIZZLE
SIZZLE
WHOA!
Where did you
come from?

My powers switched off just as suddenly as they'd switched on. I should have been exhausted, but I was still shocked from the encounter. Those two kids — they weren't there, and **THEN THEY WERE**! And there was that giggle again.

"The invisible thieves!" I breathed out loud. "There are two of them!" Somehow, my powers had bumped into their force fields (all right, so maybe I had listened to Joe's techno-babble a bit) and made them visible! And then they'd vanished again at the same time as my powers.

I rubbed my head, feeling suddenly fearful. These invisible kids . . . were they the reason my powers weren't working properly? How were they doing it?

A siren blared, and I remembered the carnival and the carousel. A cold sick feeling gripped my stomach and pain stabbed my head. Green goo. Invisibility. **Macavity**. My loss of control. Disaster!

Had I gone too far this time?

CHAPTER 10

It took a lot of courage to wipe my face and walk out into the street again. I could hear sirens. Had I hurt people on the carousel? If I had injured anyone — I couldn't bear to think about anything worse — I'd have to hand myself over to the police. I couldn't control myself. I was a danger to the people around me.

I almost turned away and went home without looking. But that would be cowardly. So I walked back toward the rides, biting my lip to stop myself from bursting into tears.

A fire truck had just arrived. As I got closer, an ambulance screeched to a halt too, closely followed by a police car. The police officer got out of the car and immediately dove into the crowd.

I was relieved to see that the carousel wasn't on fire. Nobody was staggering around bleeding everywhere. Nobody was screaming. In fact people looked mostly stunned and shocked, rather than injured. A couple of children were crying. The poor carousel owner looked devastated. Smoke oozed out of the motor in the central column, and every single light bulb in the canopy had shattered.

"Holly, there you are!" Imogen ran toward me, arms outstretched. "Are you OK?" She hugged me. "You were near that side, weren't you — what happened?"

"*I* did," I said quietly. "*I* happened."

"Oh no . . .," she said.

Joe found us a few minutes later on a bench. "Was it you?" he asked in a low voice, and his face was serious.

I just nodded.

"We have to do something about this, Holly," he told me.

"I know, I know," I said miserably. "You'd better tell them. I'm losing control. I don't know what's happening to me. I found our invisible thieves though."

Imogen and Joe both went, "**WHAT?**" at the same moment, which might have been funny in another situation.

"They were in the alley I ran down," I said. "My powers made them visible, I dunno how. They got a big shock."

Imogen looked horrified. "You *electrocuted* them?"

"No!" I said hastily. "No, no! I mean, they were shocked to see me. Not literally electrified. No, I didn't do anything like that — my powers were running out."

"Probably just as well," Joe observed dryly.

"I know," I said. "Is anyone . . . Did I . . .?"

He sat down next to me. "Look, no one was seriously injured. It was like the time you blew up the classroom. Lots of bangs and flashes and nothing serious. A few cuts and scrapes."

"What about the man who owns the carousel?" I asked miserably.

"He has insurance," Joe said reassuringly. "And if he doesn't, Steve's department will make sure he's all right, I'm sure."

"It's not their job to clean up after me."

"Um, hello?" asked Joe. "That's exactly their job!" He gave me an awkward pat on the back. "We'll figure this out, Holly, don't worry."

It's **SOOO** embarrassing being comforted by your younger brother. Imogen did it better, putting her arm around me and giving me a squeeze. "Maybe we've both got uncontrolled superpowers," she commented, trying to sound cheerful. "You're going to blow up stuff without any warning, and I'll have an invisible hand."

Joe let out a groan. "That would be *all* I need, *two* superheroes to look after. I'm going to ask for an assistant. It's so unfair! How come *I* never get any of the cool stuff? Maybe I should just go back down the beach and drink up all that green goo."

"Ewwww," said Imogen.

"You can't," I pointed out. "**POWERS** probably cleaned it up by now."

He scowled. "Typical. I never have any fun."

"Um, hello?" I said. "You have a *Gadget!* That's like geek heaven for you."

A police officer came to talk to some people nearby, and all three of us froze.

"We should move a bit farther away," Imogen said quietly. "If we stay here, someone will ask us if we saw what happened."

We got up to go, but my legs suddenly gave way and I clutched at the wall. "Whoa . . ."

"Holly!" Imogen grabbed my arm and helped steady me. "Are you all right?"

I wasn't all right. My head felt all swimmy, and I thought I might be about to puke. "I'm fine," I lied. "Just got up too fast." And then . . .

I sank down against the wall, my aching head in my hands. "I think . . . I need to sit down . . .," I said, fuzzily.

"No, you don't," I heard my brother say. "Not here. We'll get you home. There are too many people here. Let's try again. For goodness' sake, try to get control, Holly. We don't want to be **ZAPPED**."

He and Imogen each put an arm around my waist and lifted me up. Then the three of us staggered away, Joe calling cheerily to the police officer, "Bit too much sun! Don't worry, our mom's a nurse!"

"Joe . . .," I mumbled, "you are such a liar . . ."

"Yeah?" he responded, his breath coming in gasps from the effort of supporting me. "Not been best friends with the truth yourself, have you, Holly?"

I did manage to do some walking, but my balance was all wrong: it felt like my legs wanted to go in a different direction than my brain was telling them to go. We made it up the hill. By the time we got to my house, we were all pouring with sweat and gasping for air.

To our collective relief, Mom wasn't there. A note on the kitchen table said:

PAINTING CARNIVAL FLOAT. CALL IF YOU NEED ME. BACK AT 6 p.m. LOVE YOU XOXO

"What time is it?" I asked faintly.

"Three thirty," said Imogen, sinking into a chair. "I think I've died."

"I'm so thirsty," Joe croaked. He fetched us all glasses of water and we sat at the table for a few minutes, breathing heavily and taking sips of water. Eventually, Joe said, "I'm going to scan you." He held up the Gadget in front of me.

"What?" I said.

"Like I didn't get to do on Fran," Joe said. "Now seems a good moment. It shouldn't hurt. Stand up for a sec."

I staggered to my feet. But it was only after he tapped the screen and a thin blue light shot out of the Gadget at me that I registered: "Hurt? It shouldn't *hurt*? Are you —"

"Shhh."

The blue light started at the top of my head and slowly swept down over my body to my feet. I didn't feel anything, thankfully. When it reached the floor, the light swept back up to the top of my head again and then snapped off. The Gadget beeped.

"It says it's collecting data," Joe reported. "You can sit down again."

Which I did. The chair creaked. I leaned my head on my arms.

"We need food," Imogen said suddenly. "Real food, not just ice cream and cotton candy."

"Good idea." Joe said, absorbed again with the Gadget. "I'm starving."

"You stay there, Holly," Imogen said kindly.

Joe mumbled something about not being my servant, but then cast a glance at my sickly face and shut up. They raided the fridge and produced ham and cheese sandwiches, a handful of cherry tomatoes, and a bag of chips for each of us.

I took three bites of the sandwich and thought I was feeling better, but then another wave of dizziness came over me, and I put it down. "Oh, Holly," Imogen said anxiously. "Maybe we should take you to the hospital?"

"No," said Joe firmly. "Definitely not." The Gadget beeped, and Joe peered at the screen. "Lots of scrolling figures. It's hard to tell what's good or not. I mean, is 13.4 a good iron level? I dunno. Oh — oh, hang on . . ." He went silent.

I lifted my head and stared at him. "What?" He didn't say anything. "What is it, Joe?"

"Hmm. Well. OK." He took a breath. "Well, it's interesting. The screen went all flashing red and stuff."

"What? Why?"

"You're not normal," Joe told me.

"Oh, for goodness' sake," I retorted, "of course I'm not normal."

"No, I mean your 'normal' isn't normal. For you. You're abnormally abnormal." The Gadget beeped again. "It says it's sending your results to **POWERS** HEADQUARTERS."

"Oh, great." I slumped.

"Joe," said Imogen hesitantly, "can it scan my hand too? You know, the one that . . ." Her voice trailed off.

"Yeah, I don't see why not." Joe turned to her. "Stand up." Again, the blue light swept down and up and turned off.

But before the Gadget could begin working through Imogen's results, something really peculiar happened. The Gadget suddenly made a completely different type of beep, and announced to the whole room: "Area secure. Incoming."

AND THEN STEVE'S HEAD POPPED UP OUT OF JOE'S WRIST.

CHAPTER 11

I don't know if it was because I was terrified or exhausted or sick or what, but I started laughing. Steve's head wasn't here by magical means, but projected into the air as a 3D hologram by the Gadget. It was totally weird. "Holly," it said, without bothering to start with "Hello."

"Hi, Steve," I giggled, tears pouring from my eyes. I waved. "Sorry, I just — you look funny."

He didn't look amused. The eyes, dark brown in real life, glared at me. "How long have you been feeling ill?"

"Oh, not long," I said. "Day or two. Only since the first incident thing, you know."

"What incident thing?" Even through an electronic filter, I could hear Steve's voice sharpen, and I wasn't laughing any more.

"Oh . . .," I said. "Um, well . . . I lost control of my powers a bit. I sort of blew up the library.

And shocked Lin and Joe and Imogen — oh, twice for Imogen, sorry."

"That's OK," Imogen whispered.

"And then today I blew up a carousel." I could feel my face getting redder and redder, and I twisted my fingers in my lap. "And sometimes I try to use my powers and . . . nothing happens."

"And you're sick?" added Steve, though it sounded more like a question.

"It's probably just a mild flu," I offered.

"Not according to the readings you've just sent me." Steve looked away from me for a moment, at something we couldn't see. "These are unstable, Holly. You need to come in."

"Come in where?"

"To **POWERS**," Steve said bluntly. "We've got a lab. We need to check you out." He blinked. "*Now* whose results am I getting?"

"Oh, sorry," Imogen said, putting her hand in the air nervously, "those are mine. I'm worried about my hand."

"Your hand? Why, what have you done to it?"

"I put it in the green goo stuff that came out of the **CyberSky** ball thing."

I thought that Steve might have a complete meltdown. "You did *WHAT*?"

"It was an **ACCIDENT!**" I added quickly. "We weren't near the hill. We were on the beach!"

"So that's what that ..." Steve broke off, shaking his head. "You kids. Honestly, you'll be the death of me. Why can't you stay out of trouble?"

"We try!" I cried, feeling I should stand up for us somehow. "At least we're not invisible and stealing things!"

Now Steve looked like he'd gone past the point of confusion and out the other side into complete blankness. "Pardon?" he said.

Joe decided it was his turn to talk. "That's true, sir. There are at least two kids in Bluehaven who can make themselves invisible. We think they're responsible for the recent crime wave."

There was a pause while Steve's disembodied head turned slowly on Joe's wrist to stare at each of us in turn. "I can see we've got a lot to catch up on," he said eventually. "I'll send a car for you at 9 a.m. sharp. Don't blow yourselves up overnight, all right?"

The head winked into blackness and Steve was gone.

"Wow," Imogen said. "That was ... intense."

"I think I'm going to be sick," I said. And I ran for the bathroom.

Mom came back from the painting session all happy and excited. "It's going to look amazing!" she said cheerfully as she came in through the front door. Then she saw me, all wrapped up on the sofa, and her expression changed. "Goodness, Holly, you look *terrible*. Are you all right?"

Now I realize it's not very superheroey to want your mom, but it was **SO** nice to see her that I may have burst into tears just a little bit. Only for a moment, mind you, but she came and hugged me and that made my eyes leak a bit more, and we'll just gloss over that bit, OK?

I didn't tell Mom what was **REALLY** going on, *obviously*. Joe and I had discussed what we should tell her, and decided on sticking to the flu story. Imogen had gone home about half an hour earlier.

Mom felt my head anxiously and then gave me some Tylenol and brought me a drink and asked me if I'd like ice cream, and all the nice mom things that you don't realize you need until you're ill. "Did you hear what happened on the boardwalk?" she gossiped as she sat down next to me. If there's one thing my mom likes more than protesting, it's a bit of local scandal. "Terrible explosion on the carousel! Some kind of electrical fault, they think. A miracle no one was hurt."

"Gosh, really?" Joe was doing a great impression of someone who didn't know anything about it. Mom would have gone nuts if we'd admitted we were actually there. We were supposed to be "staying away from drama," remember? Hahaha.

"That's not the worst thing though," Mom went on, tutting like some old grandma. "In the chaos, while everyone was running around panicking, some terrible person picked all their pockets! Phones and wallets and all kinds of things went missing!"

Now I really was interested. "Really? Do they know who did it?"

Mom shook her head. "They're blaming the same kid who's been stealing from the shops. It could have been anyone, though, there was such a mess. That's why I always keep my wallet in my front pocket." She tapped her jeans smugly.

I caught Joe's eye and nodded. The invisible thieves, no doubt. Was it just the two of them?

I itched to get out there and chase them down. Surely with my powers and Joe's special Gadget-scanning capabilities, we'd be able to find them no problem!

But I wasn't in control of my powers, and I was hardly in control of my own digestive system either. I sighed in frustration.

"I don't know what to do about tomorrow," Mom said, her brow furrowing as she looked at me. "I was going to go to the preschool rehearsal. They need help practicing their little songs. They're so excited. They've got actions to go with the songs and everything, Nicky says. But the group is meeting at 9 a.m." She put a hand on my forehead. "I don't want to leave you if you're not well."

I was alarmed. Mom absolutely had to be out of the way if we were going to **POWERS** tomorrow. "I'm sure I'll feel better in the morning," I said, mustering the energy to produce a reassuring smile. "You know I don't really get sick much."

"I know." Mom smiled back. "You're the healthiest child I know — it must be all that physical activity you do!"

"Hello . . .," said Joe. "I'm right here."

"*You're* not healthy," Mom told him. "You get at least two throat infections a year. It's because you spend so much time holed up in your room with your video camera and the curtains drawn."

Joe opened his mouth to protest and then closed it again. Instead he said, "It's all right, Mom. I'll stay with Holly tomorrow. We can call you if she gets worse or anything."

"Really?" Mom hesitated. "Let's see how you are in the morning then."

In the morning of course, I did my best acting ever — honestly, they should give me an Oscar, I was that convincing. I snuck some of Mom's foundation makeup out of the bathroom and smoothed it onto my face so that I didn't look so pale. And then I smiled brightly and bounced down the stairs (feeling utterly sick at every step) and said, "Morning! I feel **SO** much better today!"

Mom left the house at ten to nine, and the moment the door closed, I collapsed onto the sofa, groaning. "I feel soooooo ill!"

There was a knock at the door, and for a moment, I thought Mom had come back for something. I was trying to drag myself back to my feet when Joe opened the door to Imogen. "Are you OK? You didn't blow up anything else? My hand isn't invisible!" she babbled.

I just moaned quietly in response. My body had started to tremble. Imogen noticed and took a step back. "Uhhhh, Holly . . . ?"

"It's all right," I said, and then . . .

FZZZZ!

KZZZZT!

WITHOUT WARNING, HOLLY'S POWERS EXPLODED OUT OF HER AGAIN!

I stared at the smashed and smoking TV screen. "Oh dear . . ."

"Oh DEAR?" fumed Joe. "That's ALL you can SAY?"

And then the doorbell rang and made us all jump. It was Maverick, grinning cheerfully as usual, though the grin slid off his face as soon as he saw the mess. "Oops," he said. "Had a little accident, huh?"

"I haven't WET myself," I snapped. My hands were shaking, even though the electricity had gone.

Mav was tapping the gadget on his own wrist that looked a bit like the one Joe had. "Requesting clean-up team to **ELECTRIGIRL** abode," he said clearly into it. "TV replacement."

I stared at him. "You're getting us a new TV?"

"Of course," he said, surprised by the question. "Can't have your mom asking questions, can we? Come and get into the car, we've got a long drive ahead of us."

Dumb with shock, we did exactly what he said, though I noticed that Joe and Imogen sat as far away from me as they could get in the sleek black car. I leaned my head against the window and closed my eyes . . .

It seemed like only moments later that the car jolted to a halt and the engine switched off. "We're here," said Mav.

I sat up and rubbed my stiff neck. Where were we, exactly? Out of the window, I could see a wide pedestrian-only street bordered by huge glassy buildings, and people walking around in suits, looking important and busy. Up ahead was a monorail — or that's what it looked like — running right through the whole place. "Is this a business park?" I asked. "Are we in London?"

"Near-ish," said Mav evasively. He helped me out of the car, since my legs were still kind of wobbly. "This way."

The building we went into was tall and shiny, just like the others on the street. But this one had no name or number on it or anything, just a symbol of a star surrounded by what looked like clouds.

"Is that the **POWERS** logo?" asked Joe.

"Yes," said Mav. "And shush. We don't use its name anywhere near the building."

The big glass doors slid silently apart to let us into the atrium, which was about twice as tall as my house, windows reaching all the way up to the top. In front of us was a row of gates, a bit like the ones you see at subway stations. Mav produced a card which he slid through a reader, and the gates opened long enough to let us into a kind of glass pod. We stood in this for a moment, waiting. "Where's the door on the other side?" asked Joe, reaching out to touch the glass.

And then a light beam swept all the way down from the ceiling to the floor, and the other side of the pod swished open. "Talk about security," I muttered. "Anyone would think I was about to blow the place up." And then I laughed, and then I stopped laughing because it wasn't remotely funny.

"Hey!" Steve came strolling across the shiny floor to meet us. "Holly, Imogen, Joe — good to see you again." He cast a brief nod at Mav. "Shall we go up?" He gestured toward a set of elevator doors at the far end of the atrium.

"Oh good," I said to myself. "Elevators."

There was one thing I was supremely grateful for: the lab was on the top floor of the building, not in the basement. In both of my run-ins with **Professor Macavity**, I had been trapped underground: first in the basement of the **⊛CyberSky** HQ, and second in an old tin mine in Cornwall. I was practically allergic to enclosed spaces now, they made me so scared.

When the elevator doors swooshed open, the first impression I had was of peace and quiet, and lots of light. I don't know about you, but "laboratory" to me means people in white coats and safety glasses, with handheld computers, and clipboards, and glass tubes with colored liquids bubbling in them.

I may have confused that last part with Joe's comics.

This was a very large room, with lots of computer terminals in it, and cupboards with shiny glass doors, and gleaming white machines, one of which looked a bit like our dishwasher. There were people there, sitting at computer terminals and looking through microscopes, but they weren't wearing lab coats. Some of them even looked a little untidy.

There was nothing at all untidy about the woman coming toward us, though. "Lin!" I exclaimed, and felt my face go completely beet red, which didn't help my headache.

"Hello," she said, nodding to the three of us. Lin didn't really do smiling; she was FAR too cool to smile. Or maybe she was still annoyed with me for blasting her with electricity up on the hillside. "Thank you for coming in. Follow me."

We followed Lin down the middle of the room, threading our way between quietly beeping machines and curious stares.

At the other end of the room was a door. Lin opened it and ushered us through — and **NOW** we were in the legit lab. I wasn't sure whether to be dismayed or relieved to see the bubbling test tubes and the people in white lab coats with handheld computers.

Straight ahead was a bed. A hospital bed. And about sixteen machines waiting around it, with wires of all colors coiling like worms out of them.

There was no one in the bed, but I could guess who it was for.

CHAPTER 12

There was a man standing at the end of the bed, smiling at me. He looked faintly familiar, though I was sure I'd never seen him before. He had black hair, graying at the temples, a high forehead, and was about the same age as my mom. "Holly Sparkes," he said cheerfully. Behind his glasses he had bright blue eyes. "It's a real pleasure to meet you."

"This is Dr. Moulford," said Steve. "He's top in his field."

"What field is that?" asked Joe curiously.

"I'll be back in a while," said Steve, ignoring Joe. He helped me onto the bed, nodded, and went out.

Dr. Moulford smiled at me. "I'm hoping we can sort out your little power problem."

"That's good," I said lamely. "I'd be very grateful."

"And Imogen," he said, turning to her. "We'll have a look at your hand afterward, OK? Don't worry, we won't forget you."

"Oh — thanks." Imogen looked as though she wasn't sure whether to be reassured or alarmed by this.

And then all the pleasantries were over, and basically it was time for me to be tested. I lay back and tried not to be nervous, but it was hard when things were clipped onto my fingers, and pads were stuck to my chest, and a needle was poked into my arm to extract blood . . .

"What's this for?" asked Joe. "Why's the machine doing that? What happens if this wiggly line drops below zero? Have you got a scanner? Can you look at Holly's cells under the microscope? Can I see? Do you know how she got her powers?"

"Joe," I said, urgently. "**JOE!**"

He turned. "What?"

"Shut up."

Imogen stood and watched in pale silence for a while, but when it appeared that I wasn't actually about to explode (or scream in pain, or anything out of a horror film), she asked if she could find a quiet corner to do some drawing.

To be honest, it was all very boring. When people weren't prodding or jabbing me, they were talking to each other over my head, using sciencey words I didn't understand. Lin had disappeared and Mav had gone too. Someone brought Joe and Imogen lunch in paper bags, but I wasn't allowed one because of the blood tests. I still felt so sick that I didn't want any food anyway.

Dr. Moulford frowned at his screen and said, "Yes. These match with the results your brother sent us. Most unusual."

"What is?" I asked.

He glanced at me kindly. "Your cells are depleted of electrons."

"Pardon?"

"Electrons carry electricity around the body," he explained. "You are missing some."

"Missing some?" I repeated, puzzled. "Where did they go?"

He raised his eyebrows. "I don't know. From what you've achieved with your powers, we'd assumed your body could create extra electrons when needed. You have been able to choose when this happens — switching your powers on and off."

I nodded. "Yes. But recently, I've just sort of blasted on and off without meaning to."

"Which means that your cells are randomly producing electrons and releasing them without the usual control from the brain," agreed Dr. Moulford. "And from what these results suggest, every time you do that, you're letting go of too many electrons. Which is why you're feeling very unwell at the moment."

"Can you fix it?" I asked hopefully. "Can you make me better?"

He smiled at me. "Ah, the words every doctor fears! I'll do my best, Holly."

"What . . .," I started nervously, "what do you think happens . . . if you can't fix it?"

He thought for a moment. "Your cells are unbalanced. This overproduction and then over-release of energy without proper control is likely to worsen. That will make you a danger to anyone around you and particularly to electrical items or resources."

"Oh," I said. "I'm kind of already a danger."

"You would be *more* of a danger."

I nodded, but you can trust my brother to ask the questions no one else wants to ask. "*How* dangerous could she get?" he wanted to know.

"Thanks, Joe," I muttered under my breath. I didn't want to know. And yet I sort of did.

"It's hard to say," Dr. Moulford replied. "But it's not too far-fetched to suggest that she could take out the main electricity grid."

Joe's eyes widened. He looked impressed.

"And that would be . . . bad, right?" I said. "Because that electricity is . . . important."

Joe buried his head in his hands. "I'm not related to her," he groaned.

"Yes, it's important," said Dr. Moulford. "Everything across the country that's plugged into the main electricity grid would be affected."

"Right . . .," I said. "I see." And I did. Because that's everything in my house, practically — TV, computers, phone, washing machine, etc. They're all plugged into that main source of electricity. And if it is a source for everyone, every single person in the country could be cut off from everything they use.

"As for what would happen to you . . .," Dr. Moulford said slowly. "The human body is immensely strong in many ways, but a release of energy that large . . . well. I think . . . you would be unlikely to survive."

I stared at him.

"Not," he added hastily, "that it will come to that. We'll find a way to stabilize you, I'm sure." He smiled at me in a reassuring way.

Oh good. So I destroy the country, and then I die? Fantastic. My gaze met Joe's and I saw shock in his eyes too. Despite all his enthusiasm for my superpowers, I don't think Joe had ever really considered the possibility that I might actually die. I was sort of pleased to see that he was upset by the idea. And I felt angry with him for asking the question in the first place.

Dr. Moulford was fiddling with one of the machines now. "Just lie back," he said. "I'm going to try to check the electrical current in your body and see if there's something we can do to stabilize it."

I did as I was told and stared up at the ceiling, which looked oddly blurry. It was one thing to be told you might be responsible for the country's collapse; yet another to be told

YOU WERE AT RISK OF ACTUAL, PERMANENT DEATH . . .

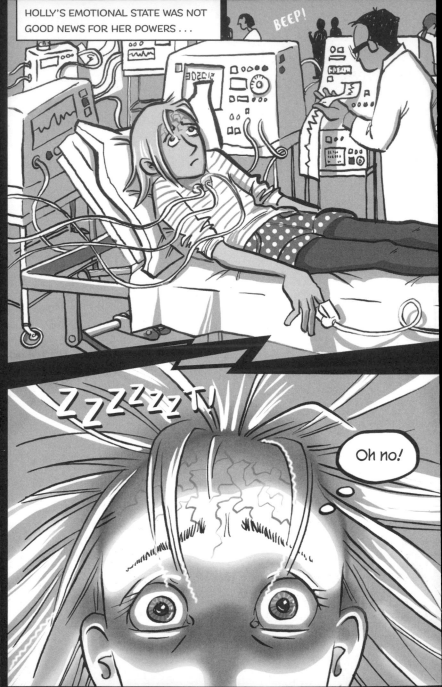

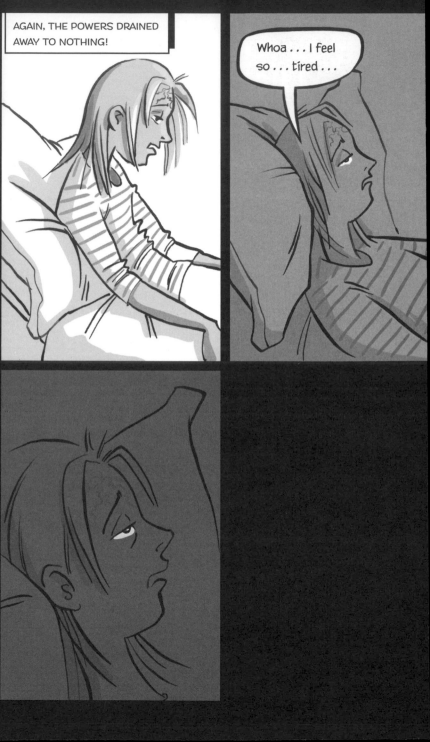

CHAPTER 13

When I came to, the first thing I registered was the high-pitched squealing of several alarms going off. I was lying on the bed again, and on opening my eyes, the first thing I saw was Lin, standing at the end of the bed and pointing an enormous gun at me. "Whoa!" I cried, putting my hands up, and nearly passing out again. "**DON'T SHOOT!**"

She didn't move.

"Oooh," I said, lowering my hands to my head instead. "Owww . . ." I tried looking around, and then wished I hadn't. The place was a mess. Shattered glass sparkled on the floor; any machine within ten feet of me was completely kaput, hidden under a layer of white foam, which someone had presumably sprayed while I was unconscious. People were talking in subdued voices, some of them carefully picking bits of glass out of their hair. A little way off, Imogen and Joe were standing together, their faces white. Weirdly, they were holding hands as they stared at me.

"Oh . . .," I said quietly. "Oh, I'm so sorry." I wasn't quite sure who I was talking to — maybe everyone.

"Welcome back," said Dr. Moulford, looking surprisingly cheerful for a man who was half-blackened by smoke and half-whitened by foam. He took off his glasses to polish them and then realized he didn't have any clean fabric to use, so put them back on again. "That was an interesting demonstration."

"I'm so sorry," I said again. "I'll pay for the damage . . ." Which was a bit ridiculous, since I never had enough money to buy ice cream, let alone the millions this lab must have cost.

He smiled at me. "You're not the first to have blown up this lab, and I'm willing to bet you won't be the last." He nodded at Lin. "You can put that down now."

Lin lowered the gun, but never took her eyes off me. Great — here I was being **SUPREMELY STUPID** in front of her again!

"The good news," Dr. Moulford continued, "is that I think I have some idea of how to stabilize your fluctuating electrical current."

"Huh?" I replied politely.

"I think I can fix you."

"Oh! Oh, that's great!"

Someone must have given Joe and Imogen a signal because they suddenly rushed over to hug me. "I'm fine," I said, a bit embarrassed. "Got a bit of a headache, but I'm not dead, am I?" Then I saw Imogen's face. "Oh, sorry, I didn't mean to joke . . ."

"I think," said Dr. Moulford, "that we should all have a cup of tea and a biscuit."

Ten minutes later we were back in the outer part of the lab, the part that looked more like an office than a lab. This section had at least escaped damage. Joe, Imogen, Dr. Moulford, and I were all sitting around a shiny table with various drinks (I had a very nice hot chocolate) and snacks. Lin stood a little way off, the gun now hooked into her belt. I had no doubt she could whip it out in less than a second if needed, so I tried not to look too electricky.

Dr. Moulford was very interested in what we had to tell him about the invisible thieves in Bluehaven. "Fascinating . . .," he said, his eyes lighting up. "And they became visible when you bumped into them, Holly?"

"I didn't get that close," I explained. "I think they got into my electrical field, kind of thing."

He agreed. "You disrupted their own force fields."

I nodded. "That's what I thought." I ignored Joe's snort of great disbelief.

Dr. Moulford misunderstood Joe's snort and turned to face him. "All vision relies on light waves," he said. "You only see something because its atoms reflect or absorb light. But if you can find a way to bend light around or pass through the atoms, the object effectively becomes invisible."

"Yes, I know," Joe said, sounding a little injured. "And if you bring a powerful electromagnet into that light-bending field, you confuse the waves, because visible light is only one little bit of the spectrum of electricity."

Dr. Moulford smiled broadly. "You know your stuff, young man. Want a job here when you grow up?"

I'd never seen my brother struck dumb before. He's not the sort of person to be short of an opinion, so it was really very funny that he completely lost the power of speech at this and simply sat motionless. His mouth kept opening and closing like a fish, and he made a faint gasping sound.

Imogen put up her hand, just like she was at school. "Um," she said. "I don't mean to interrupt, but . . . about my hand?"

Dr. Moulford said, "Ah! Yes! Well, I can't scan it here because the scanner . . . needs repair. But we can go down a couple of levels to the manufacturing department. They have the right kind of machine there." He glanced at me. "How do you feel, Holly? You can stay here and rest if you like."

"No way," I said, pushing back my chair and pretending I felt **JUST PEACHY** (one of those silly things Mom's friend Nicky says). "I'm coming too."

Lin got into the elevator with us, just in case I had any ideas about blowing stuff up again. I tried not to look at her. Though I did catch another glimpse of the big gun she was carrying, and was slightly more relieved to see that it seemed to be a tranquillizer gun, rather than the kind that had bullets.

Three floors down the elevator went "**PING**" and we got out to face a neat little sign that said: **MANUFACTURING**. "Through here," said Dr. Moulford, pushing open double doors.

"Cool," breathed Joe, who had regained the power of actual words.

We were inside a long room. Strip lights ran along the full length of the ceiling, and the floor was sectioned off into workstations. People were busy in each section. The one nearest us was doing something with a complicated wooden structure about the size of a beach ball. It looked like one of those fiendish wooden puzzles people give you for Christmas because they hope it'll keep you occupied for hours so you won't bother them. I couldn't imagine what it was for.

"Follow me," Dr. Moulford said. "And don't touch anything."

I didn't need to be told twice. As we passed the counter tops, I could see all manner of sharp and pointy tools, as well as the kind you plug in and they whizz around and cut through metal. Oh, and blowtorches. There was no way I was going to touch ANY of these, and I wondered at Dr. Moulford's wisdom in bringing me down here. This was *so* not the kind of room you should bring an erratic human battery into . . .

Joe kept making little hiccupping noises of delight as he looked around. One bench was covered in tiny circuit boards and pieces that looked like metal building block pieces. "I bet this is where my Gadget was made," he whispered to me.

Eventually we reached the right workstation. This one was almost painfully tidy, with the few items on it set in neat, obsessive rows. There was a large shiny white machine sitting on top of the counter, flat and rectangular: something that looked a bit like a household scanner.

"Dr. Sugden," said Dr. Moulford, "may we borrow your scanner? I need to put Imogen's hand into it."

A young woman turned around. She had a nice round face, freckles, and short glossy brown hair. She also had a huge pair of goggles on, which she lifted up and snapped onto the top of her head. "Sure, Bill!" she said. "What's happened to her hand?"

"We don't know yet," Dr. Moulford said. "But we can't use the scanner upstairs because it's broken."

"Broken?" asked Dr. Sugden, staring. "How?"

"I accidentally blew it up," I admitted.

Dr. Sugden looked at me and nodded, impressed. "I know who you are," she said with a grin. "Good to meet you, **ELECTRIGIRL**."

"Oh! Thanks," I said, feeling a mixture of pride and embarrassment. How did she know who I was? Was I a sort of celebrity here?

Dr. Moulford lifted up the lid of the scanner and pressed a button. As we watched, the machine suddenly expanded upward like an unfolding accordion. "Set your hand in this slot," Dr. Moulford told Imogen.

She looked a bit nervous, and I didn't blame her. "Will it hurt?"

"Oh, no!" he said with a smile. "It might feel a bit warm, I suppose."

"Tingly," added Dr. Sugden cheerfully. "I've scanned my own hands — and my feet, actually. It's perfectly safe." She waved both her hands at us, in a kind of jazz-hands way. Then she did a little tap dance. I stared. She grinned at me, winked, pulled her goggles back over her eyes, and returned to her work.

Imogen slid her hand into the slot in the machine, and Dr. Moulford pressed a few buttons. A bright light shone out of the side, like a photocopier. And then it went out.

"All done!" said Dr. Moulford.

Imogen withdrew her hand, surprised. "Is that it?"

Dr. Moulford tapped on the scanner again. "I'm sending the results upstairs," he said. "There are a few machines Holly didn't manage to destroy. I'll analyze everything upstairs." He smiled at the three of us. (Joe jumped, having been caught trying to sneak a look at another workstation.) "You want to come back upstairs with me?"

"Wait up!" called a familiar voice, and we turned to see Mav jogging toward us. Lin gave a tiny sigh. Mav beamed when he reached us. "How's it going? Steve will join soon, but he said I can show you the fabric construction section."

"The what?" I asked.

But Joe was practically hopping from foot to foot. "Suits!" he almost yelled. "Superhero outfits!"

I laughed. "Joe, don't be stupid. They don't have a Superhero Costume department." Then I glanced at Mav. "Do you?"

He grinned. "Wanna see?"

CHAPTER 14

"This is **ALL MY DREAMS** come true," breathed Joe, as we headed for the double doors at the end of the room. Dr. Moulford had headed off in the opposite direction. Joe's eyes were wide so as not to miss a single moment, and his face was a picture of total ecstasy. "You guys have other superheroes working for you, don't you? You can tell me. I won't tell."

"That's classified," Lin said crisply.

"Are the invisible kids working for you?" asked Joe suddenly. "I mean, you must have known about them, right? You've probably got a database or something of superhumans."

Mav exchanged a look with Lin. "Uh . . ."

"That's classified too," said Lin.

"You *didn't* know about them, did you?" said Joe smugly. "Have we discovered two brand-new enhanced humans?"

But the other two were saved from having to answer by what was on the other side of the doors . . .

I stared. We were in a corridor lined with clothes, but these clothes looked as though they had serious purposes. There were all-in-one biohazard suits, camouflage outfits, thin black leotards, saris, burkas, fur-lined sealskin coats . . .

"We have to make sure we stock outfits for any kind of environment," Lin commented as she strode along ahead of us. "And sometimes we get special requests." She opened another door. "Like the one in here."

This was a very small room. There was only one outfit hanging on the wall. And my eyes grew bigger and bigger as I stared at it, and my tummy was flipping like an overexcited dolphin.

"That's what I drew . . .," breathed Imogen, and Joe grabbed my arm, speechless.

"Yes, your designs were very helpful," Lin said. "What do you think?"

"Do I . . . um . . .," I said, swallowing, "do I get to try it on?"

"Yes," Lin said. She unhooked the hanger. "There's a restroom at the end of the corridor out there. Go put it on and come back here. They're working on a belt for you too."

The fabric felt really strange under my fingers, almost silky. But it stretched too, like spandex. What was it made of? I got changed in the bathroom stall, banging my elbow on the door twice (these places are never big enough!) and thinking that **POWERS** may well be a super top secret whatnot of a place, but they didn't have decent changing rooms! The fabric clung to my skin, but not in an uncomfortable way; more as though it were actually part of it. There was a mask too that molded to my head and hid my scar completely. I wondered how they'd managed to get all my measurements so exactly right.

As I pulled the last seam into place, I felt a thrill run through me,

LIKE MY USUAL TINGLE BUT MUFFLED . . .

CHAPTER 15

When I changed out of my suit, the muffled tingling vanished, which was partly a disappointment and partly a relief. I hoped that Dr. Moulford would have a solution by the time we went home today.

Imogen and Joe were still grinning when I came out of the restroom, the suit draped over my arm. "You looked so cool," Imogen said. "I can't believe I'm friends with a real superhero."

I laughed. "You still can't believe it? It's been months!"

"I know," she said, "but somehow, when you put the costume on . . ."

"Suit," I said firmly. "It's a suit. A super-suit."

Joe was looking at me with his head on one side. "You look taller," he observed.

Mav glanced at his wrist. "We should get back up to the lab. See if Imogen's results are in."

In the elevator on the way back up, I held Imogen's hand tightly. She was trembling a bit. "You're going to be fine," I whispered to her.

"What if I'm not, Holly?" she whispered back. "How . . . how will I tell my mom?"

Dr. Moulford beamed as he saw us approach. He was working in a corner of the first room, the desk covered in bits of tiny gadgety-looking stuff (what? I told you, I don't do technobabble) and had the same kind of goggles on as Dr. Sugden did downstairs. "Did you like the outfit?"

"Suit," I repeated. "It's a suit. And it's amazing."

He nodded. "Pretty pleased with that one. Some of the others haven't gone quite so well."

"Others?" Joe's ears pricked up. "*Other* super-suits? For *other* superheroes?"

Dr. Moulford caught sight of Lin behind us, and his expression glazed over. "Oh. Ah . . . hmmm. Where did I put that screwdriver?" He coughed and then said, "The good news is we haven't found anything to worry about in the scan of Imogen's hand."

Beside me, Imogen slumped with relief.

"Though," Dr. Moulford continued, "it's not *entirely* normal either."

"Not normal?" Imogen tensed up again. "What do you mean?"

"Difficult to say exactly," Dr. Moulford mused, applying the tiny screwdriver to a screw no bigger than a pin. "The molecules seem a little . . . fluid."

"Fluid?" I repeated. "You mean . . . like water?"

"My hand is made of water?" Imogen asked, bewildered.

"No, no!" Dr. Moulford said quickly. "Nothing like that. The walls of the cells are a little . . . thin, shall we say? But it might just be temporary. Joe can scan it every day and send the results to us. That'll let us know if there's anything to worry about. Forget about it for the moment."

He snapped a tiny piece of black plastic onto the item he was holding, and said, "All right. Let's try this beauty out."

Then, before I knew it, he was out from behind the desk, over to me, and pressing the tiny black item to the back of my neck, just under my hairline. There was a sharp pain.

"Ow!" I jcrked away, feeling for the back of my neck. The object was firmly stuck there. "What . . . what is it?"

"Electron stabilizer," Dr. Moulford said, nodding as though pleased with himself. "It should stop you releasing electricity willy-nilly."

"Thanks," I said, hesitantly. "You really think it'll work?"

He smiled at me. "I really do. Why not try it out?"

"Here? Are you sure?"

"I have full confidence in my technology," Dr. Moulford said with a twinkle in his eye.

I glanced around at the others. Joe and Imogen looked nervous, and I couldn't blame them. "Well . . . all right . . ." I took a deep breath and composed myself.

THEN I CLOSED MY EYES AND CONCENTRATED . . .

I couldn't believe how relieved I felt when I switched off my powers without any further explosions. I could see Joe and Imogen were relieved too.

On an impulse, I held out my hand to Dr. Moulford. He shook it, grinning. "Thank you," I said. "Thank you." I couldn't express how grateful I was, really. This tiny thing, whatever it was, was going to save my life. And stop me from destroying all of the country's electricity of course. But mostly I was just glad I was going to live.

We said goodbye to Dr. Moulford and headed back down to the ground floor. I was suddenly extremely hungry. My headache had gone away and I felt almost like myself again. "Hi!" I said, as we stepped out of the elevator and saw Steve waiting for us.

He grinned at me. "You look better. I hear I have a hefty repair bill."

"Sorry, Steve," I said. "Um, do you know if there are any snacks around?"

Steve turned to Mav. "Go and get Holly a lunch bag from the canteen."

Mav said airily, "Oh, we'll stop at a drive-through on the way home." Steve just stared at him, and Mav coughed and said, "So, yeah, I could get her a bag. Just to keep her going." Then he took a few steps backward, like he was trying to leave without losing face, gave me a professional-looking nod, and scurried off.

"He can't help it," Lin said to Steve. "He's incapable of following instructions."

"All right," said Steve to the three of us. "I've got a mission for you."

"Macavity?" Joe said enthusiastically.

"No," said Steve, and I felt slightly relieved. "No, let us keep an eye on her. She's got powerful friends; you don't want to cross her until we know what she's really up to. Your job should be right up your alley — literally. The streets and people of Bluehaven are plagued by a crime wave, I hear." He winked.

"The invisible thieves!" Imogen exclaimed. "We were sort of on that mission anyway!"

Steve nodded. "Well, now you're on it officially. We think the children may have been contaminated by the green liquid from the **CyberSky** tower. That may be how they got their powers, but we won't know for sure until they come in and we can run some tests. We need to make sure their powers are stable."

"And give them a good talking-to," said Imogen, looking upset. "They're breaking the law!"

"That too," said Steve, seriously. "They're using their powers for personal gain, which is not acceptable. They could do with a good mentor, I expect."

Joe coughed very loudly.

"*You* can't mentor them," I told him. "You're *my* mentor."

"Yeah," he said, "and look how much you listen to me!"

"Well, you need to listen to your mentor now," Steve told me, and his tone sounded a bit stern. "We want you to find the children and talk to them. If you show them your powers, they may be more willing to talk to you and agree to come in to **POWERS**. Joe will receive instructions from us through the KX24-C."

"The wh— oh, the Gadget!"

"And you need to *follow* those instructions," Steve said pointedly. "I want daily scans of you and Imogen so that we can monitor your stability. Any progress you make on the invisible thieves, you message in immediately. Understand?"

"Yes, sir," said Joe importantly.

Steve grinned at me. "Your powers can disrupt an invisible force field. You're probably the best agent **POWERS** can send on this mission. You up for it?"

I felt pride and excitement flood through me. "You bet I am!"

"GO GET 'EM, ELECTRIGIRL!"

CHAPTER 16

We got home five minutes before Mom did, which was very lucky because we didn't have a backup plan for being late. I just had time to jump onto the sofa with a blanket as she bustled in through the front door. "I'm so sorry, I meant to be back in time to make you lunch, and now it's nearly three!" she exclaimed. She dumped her bag on the floor and hurried over to me, feeling my forehead and examining my face. "How do you feel?" She drew back, surprised. "Actually, you're looking better."

"Yeah," I said, crossing my fingers at the lie I was about to tell. "A day on the sofa has definitely helped."

She beamed at me. "That's great. And I'm home just in time, because I received a text from your Dad half an hour ago . . ." The phone rang. "That'll be him now!" She practically leaped across the room for the phone. "Hello? Hello, darling, how are you?"

There's a special voice my mom only uses when she's on the phone with my dad. It's like she suddenly goes all soft and young. It's kind of sweet really. I like that they're so pleased to hear from each other. Sometimes it feels like we're a one-parent family, since Dad is away with the army so much. I don't really miss Dad too bad, because that's just how our life is — but when he calls, I suddenly remember how much fun he is and how much I'd like him to come home again.

When it was my turn, I took the phone from Mom and settled on the sofa. "Hi, Dad."

"Hi, Mini-Spark," came his familiar voice, and I grinned. His friends in the army call him Sparky because of our last name, and when I was little, I had so much energy, he started calling me Mini-Spark. "How's it going?"

"Good, thanks," I said, trying to think what I could tell him. My visit to **POWERS** — nope. My mission to catch invisible thieves — nope. The super-suit currently squashed into a bag at the bottom of my dresser — double nope. "I've been eating a lot of ice cream." Lame but true.

He chuckled. "Do they still do that blackberry cheesecake flavor at the kiosk?"

"Yes," I said. "And they've added chocolate cherry brownie this year too. And mango sorbet."

"Oooh." I could practically hear him drooling. "I could handle one of those where I am now."

"Are you in the desert again?" I asked sympathetically.

I heard him sigh. "No, not exactly. Wish I could tell you where, Mini-Spark. Your eyes would pop out of your head."

I knew he couldn't tell me where he was. It was an army rule. "When are you coming home, Dad?"

There was a short pause. "It was supposed to be next month," he said. "But it looks like I might be out here for a bit longer. There's something they want me to do."

"Can't someone else do it?" I asked, feeling disappointed. "You've been away for forever."

"I know. But I've got certain skills. I'm one of a kind, Mini-Spark." He laughed. "But I promise you I'll be home before Christmas. I'm not missing another one of those!"

"Is that Dad?" Joe rushed into the room, holding out his hand. "My turn, my turn."

As always when I finished talking to Dad, I felt kind of sad and tummy-achy. It was so nice to hear his voice, but he still wasn't here.

The next morning, Joe burst into my room waving a pair of ancient walkie-talkies that he'd been given for his sixth birthday. "**LOOK WHAT I FOUND**!"

I yawned. "Congratulations. Go away."

He came close and whispered, "They're perfect for hunting our invisible thieves."

Suddenly I was wide awake.

We met up with Imogen at eleven o'clock. Mom wanted to do a big grocery trip, so she drove us down the hill into town and made us promise to be home in time for lunch.

"There are only two walkie-talkies," Imogen pointed out. "So we can't all have one."

Joe nodded. "Holly should have one, obviously. She's the only one who can make the invisible thieves visible. I'll keep the other, and you and me will go hunting together. If we see something suspicious, we'll radio Holly and she can come and electrify them."

"What kind of suspicious?" Imogen asked.

"I'll be scanning the area," Joe said importantly. "I'll let you know if the number of heat signals on the Gadget doesn't match the number we can see."

Imogen looked underwhelmed. "Am I supposed to just stand around waiting then?"

"Of course not," I said, shooting an annoyed look at my brother. "You'll be looking out for the same things I am: a shimmer in the air, someone being bumped into and looking puzzled, things falling over for no reason. Or maybe a sound that comes out of the air — a cough or a giggle or something."

She nodded a little more brightly. "OK, I can do that. Are you wearing your costume under your clothes, Holly? Like Superman?"

"It's a *suit*," I said. Why couldn't anyone get it right? "And no, I'm not. I'd be way too hot."

"Oh, good point," said Imogen, nodding. "I wonder if that's why we never see him going to the beach. Superman, I mean. And it's never hot in Metropolis, is it? Which is good because that spandex would get awfully sweaty."

"When you've *quite* finished," Joe said sarcastically, "we have a job to do."

I took the walkie-talkie. "Shall we do the boardwalk first? I could take one end, you could take the other. We could meet in the middle."

"The end with the fairground is still roped off," said Joe. He caught sight of my expression. "Um, Imogen and I will take that end. You start at the other, OK?"

It was a cloudy day with quite a strong breeze and not all that warm, but the forecast was good so the beach was already filling up with people. I passed a poster pasted to a lamp post, advertising the Bluehaven Carnival. The image was of a woman in a huge peacock costume, smiling as she danced. Someone had added glasses and a moustache to the photo. I moved out of the way as a family crossed the boardwalk and climbed down the steps to the beach. The parents were bickering: "I left it with you." "Well, you should have said something. How was I supposed to know it was there?"

The older brother glanced at me as he passed and rolled his eyes. I gave him a sympathetic smile.

My walkie-talkie suddenly crackled into life. "Thunderbolt calling **ELECTRIGIRL**!" came Joe's excited voice. "We just found something! Between Lucy's Café and the flag."

"On my way," I said, already setting off at a sprint.

Imogen and Joe were standing beside Lucy's Café. Where the wall met the concrete surface of the boardwalk, there was a downpipe from the gutter. Tucked behind the gutter was a collection of clothes. "If you wanted to hide someone's clothes as a prank," Joe said, "wouldn't this be a good place to put them?"

I frowned. "But you'd hang around, wouldn't you? To see what happened?" My gaze swept the area. "Did you pick them up on the Gadget?"

Joe looked bashful. "Well — no. To be honest, it's difficult to see whether the moving blobs on the Gadget screen match up to the moving people around us. Especially when it's this busy."

"I found the clothes," Imogen said proudly.

I grinned at her. Gadget, shmadget. Eyes, that's all we needed!

Just then two people came clambering up the steps from the beach. There was a tall, very thin man, and a shorter woman with long dark hair that was dripping down her back. Both were wearing swimsuits, wrapped in towels, and both were very red in the face. "I can't drive back like this," the man was complaining.

The woman shook her head. "I bet it's kids. Got no discipline, that's the problem." She glanced at us and scowled. "Parents let them get away with anything." Her eyes slid over me, and landed on the downpipe of the café. Her mouth fell open and she stopped. The man bumped into her. "That's our clothes!" she cried. Pushing past me and Imogen, she reached for them, pulling out a long blue skirt, a white blouse, pink underwear, and bra. "Yours are here too!"

"What? But how did they get there?" the man exclaimed.

The woman turned on us, furious. "Stealing people's clothes like this is not funny. **WHO DO YOU THINK YOU ARE**?"

"It wasn't us!" protested Joe, but my attention was caught by a small sound. A familiar giggle. The invisible kids! I glanced sharply to my left, but saw no one. There was a faint shimmer in the air though, and the instincts in my body kicked in.

POWER FLOODED THROUGH MY BODY . . .

I let my powers fade for the moment. Being on high alert without an idea of the location of the thieves could be dangerous — for me, and for everyone around me. I didn't want to start giving random strangers electric shocks! "No," I replied into the walkie-talkie, disappointed. "I lost them . . ."

Then something caught my eye and I turned my head. "**WAIT!** I think I saw a shimmer!"

Had I imagined it? Just outside the costume shop . . . had there been a movement in the air? Or was I seeing things? I shook my head. Trying to spot invisible people made your eyes play tricks on you!

"Where are you?" came Joe's voice through the walkie-talkie.

"Outside the glove shop," I said, distracted. What if it *had* been a real shimmer? The door of the costume shop was open, so anyone could walk in. I'd better make sure. "I'm just going to check it out," I told Joe, and then slipped the walkie-talkie onto my belt.

"We're on our way!" crackled Joe's voice excitedly. I felt a bit guilty. By the time they got here, I'd probably be apologizing for the false alarm.

The costume shop, Fancy Dress Startdust Shop, had been in Bluehaven as long as I could remember, and so had Mr. Pyper, the owner. If you wanted a pair of silly glasses, or a fake nose, or a full-length ostrich outfit, you went to Pyper's. The inside of the shop was like a huge walk-in closet, with racks and racks of costumes for all occasions. He also sold wigs, and Joe had once heard a rumor that Mr. Foley, the mayor, bought his from there, though Mr. Pyper firmly denied it.

"Holly!" said Mr. Pyper as I went in. "Sorry, dear, I'm just about to step out for a sandwich. Is it something I can help you with quickly before I lock up? Otherwise you'll have to come back in about ten minutes. Or twenty, depending on the line at the bakery." He grinned.

"Oh . . .," I said, wondering what to do. "I, um . . ."

The walkie-talkie in my belt crackled suddenly. "Holly," came my brother's voice, "where are —"

CLICK! I switched it off, since Mr. Pyper was looking surprised. "Sorry!" I said with a smile. "Playing . . . spies. Yes, spies!" I was quite pleased to have thought up a good excuse so quickly.

Mr. Pyper chuckled. "You kids. Wish I was still young enough to play those kinds of games. I'm just going to grab my wallet, and then I'll help you find what you need if it's quick."

He went through the curtain to the back room and I had only seconds to decide on my course of action. What should I do?

And then I heard a faint giggle, and I knew that they were here!

Footsteps approached from the back room, and I dashed behind a nearby clothes rack, using a royal-looking robe to hide myself.

"Holly?" I heard Mr. Pyper say in a puzzled tone. The footsteps moved across the shop floor and hesitated. I held my breath. Then they started up again, and Mr. Pyper went out of the shop door, pulling it shut behind him. I heard a key turn in the lock.

PHEW! But before I could move, I heard that giggle again and a lot of rustling. Carefully I peeked through the armhole of the robe.

Even though I knew there were two invisible children in front of me, I couldn't see them at all. What I *could* see was a bunch of clothes dancing about in the air. The kids were clearly pulling things off racks and waving them around. A grass skirt suddenly disappeared — and then a striped waistcoat. I remembered that when anything got too close to the children's skin, it became invisible too, swallowed up by their force field.

I couldn't believe what I was seeing. The kids were making a total mess of the place! Mr. Pyper would only be gone for ten minutes, and then he'd return to find his shop in chaos! I gritted my teeth. These children had no respect for anything!

It was time to intervene.

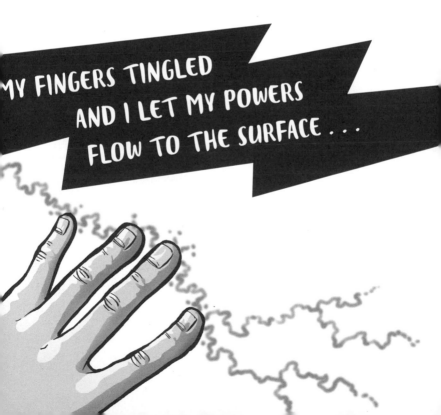

MY FINGERS TINGLED AND I LET MY POWERS FLOW TO THE SURFACE . . .

THE BLINK OF AN EYE, THE CHILDREN HAD MADE THEMSELVES INVISIBLE AGAIN!
Smell you later!
Oh no you don't! See, I'm not what you think . . .
How are you doing that?
Hey! Leave us alone!

CHAPTER 17

I WAS ARRESTED. Well, sort of. When the fire department showed up, they saw me standing alone inside a locked shop that was on fire, and at first they thought I was the victim of an accident. But when they'd put out all the flames, they decided that the number of small fires had been started individually (which of course was true), and that I must have been responsible (which was also true), and that I must have been stupid enough not to realize I was locked in (not in the least true) . . . and then the police showed up and took me to the station. Poor Mr. Pyper was absolutely devastated. "Why, Holly, why?" he kept wailing, and I felt **TERRIBLE**. I mean, I hadn't actually burned down the shop, but quite a lot of costumes were reduced to ashes, or melted, and it didn't take a genius to guess they'd be difficult to replace.

I'm guessing Dylan and Sasha sneaked out when the doors were opened. I didn't see a shimmer or anything. I was still numb with shock. The twins had met **Professor Macavity**. How had I not connected them to her before? It was obvious! They had been contaminated by the green goo, and there were any number of ways it could have happened. The liquid was **CyberSky**'s, and Dylan and Sasha must have the right kind of DNA. How long would they go unnoticed by the woman who invented the stuff?

Macavity's ambition was world domination, and who *wouldn't* want invisible spies working for them? If you were invisible, you could get into banks, governments, defense systems . . .

The police called Mom, who arrived looking pale and frightened. "Holly, what have you been doing?"

It was a very uncomfortable interview. The police were genuinely confused as to why I would start fires inside a locked shop — but I was the only suspect, so they couldn't imagine how else it could have happened. How could I possibly tell them I'd deliberately gotten myself locked into the shop because I was chasing invisible thieves? And that the fires had been an accidental side effect of using my powers to try to catch them?

There was just NO WAY, was there? And I couldn't think of ANYTHING that would be a believable excuse. I'm not good with imagination. Joe and Imogen are the ones who can think stuff up quickly. So I said nothing. Nothing at all.

And eventually even Mom's patience ran out and she threw up her hands and apologized to the police that her daughter was behaving so poorly, which made me feel **AWFUL**. The police said since I'd never been in trouble before, they wouldn't do anything serious right now. But I was given a stern talking-to, and told that a letter would be sent to my teacher, Mrs. Lester.

It's fair to say that I wasn't feeling all that great by the time Mom and I emerged into the sunlight, and she was even angrier because all the frozen food from her grocery trip had defrosted in the trunk of her car. She was so mad that she didn't speak to me all the way home, and when we got back, she just said, "Go to your room. I don't want to see you until dinner time."

"Where's Joe?" I dared to ask.

But Mom turned her back on me.

All right so I may have done a bit of crying when I got to my room. I felt like I'd messed everything up. But what else could I have done? It was my *job* to go after the twins. I was *supposed* to use my powers against them. And in fact I *had* successfully managed to use them in a private space where no members of the public could see. It had worked — the twins had appeared when I hit their force fields with my electricity. I had been in full control, thanks to the electron stabilizer.

It was just a shame that I'd set fire to the shop.

When I finished crying, I sat up and stared at the wall. I had to admit, maybe I hadn't handled the talking part very well. Dylan and Sasha thought I was telling them off for stealing things (which, all right, I was), and then when I discovered they were "friends" with **Macavity**, I probably didn't say the right things then either.

Maybe I should be a superhero who uses her powers without ever saying a single word, since it was the talking that got me into trouble . . .

It was about half an hour later that I heard the front door open and Joe come thumping up the stairs. "You're not to talk to your sister!" I heard Mom shout, but Joe ignored her and came straight in. "Holy BATMAN, she's annoying," he groaned.

"Mom?" I asked, confused.

"No, Nicky! That's where I've been for the past three hours! When you went off to the police station, Mom called Nicky and got her to pick me up and take me back to her place. You have *no idea* what I've endured." He sank dramatically onto the end of my bed.

"What *you've* endured?" I snapped. "How'd you like being interviewed by the police?"

His eyes gleamed. "I'd *love* it! Were you taken into one of those rooms that's completely bare except for a table and a couple of chairs? Did they record your interview? Did they shine a lamp in your face? Were there two of them — did they do good cop/bad cop?"

I stared at him. "This isn't TV."

He suddenly looked alarmed. "You didn't tell them anything, did you?"

"Of course not!"

He held up a hand. "Hang on. Let's start at the beginning. Why did you set fire to the costume shop?"

"Because the twins were in there! Obviously. And I didn't mean to set fire to the shop . . .," I trailed off, miserably. "That poor shop owner. He must have been so shocked when he came back with his sandwich."

Joe patted me sympathetically (and annoyingly) on the shoulder. "It's all right," he said. "I can tell you're traumatized. Even superheroes are allowed to have deep emotional angst, you know. And moral questions about right and wrong. Look at Captain America, for example."

I blinked. "I don't have deep emotional angst. Or moral issues. What are you talking about?"

He stared at me. "Well, didn't you lose control of your powers again? I assumed you were pondering your very existence as an enhanced human."

"Joe, sometimes you talk like a book," I retorted. "You're so wrong, you're on **PLANET WRONG**."

"What happened then?"

"Dylan and Sasha happened. That's their names. They were horsing around with the costumes."

He frowned. "Dylan and Sasha, twins? I think they go to my school."

Now I was the one to stare at him. "They go to your *school*? You're kidding me!"

"I'm not. I think they're in the year below me. I've seen them on the playground."

"Well, they're the invisible thieves. I tried to talk to them," I said.

Joe groaned. "Oh no. I know what's coming. Holly, we have to work on your communication skills."

"They were rude!" I said defensively. "And besides, we've got more to worry about than my communication skills. They . . . oh, Joe . . . they said they've been offered a job. By **Macavity**."

"*What?*" His face turned pale. "No way."

"She told them they could be super-spies, or something. Jewel thieves. They were all excited about it. They said when she's mayor, everything will change."

"Everything will change?" Joe repeated slowly. "What does that mean?"

"I don't know," I said. "But it can't be good."

CHAPTER 18

Well then, this was it. This was what being a superhero really meant. I stood in front of the mirror and looked at myself. I was wearing my suit, the one Imogen and **POWERS** had designed. There was a narrow belt now too. It felt . . . right. Powerful. But controlled, thanks to the electron stabilizer. There were still butterflies in my tummy though.

It was the day of the Bluehaven Carnival, and also the day the new mayor would be announced. There was no question about it: **ELECTRIGIRL** needed to be there. Mom was having none of it, of course. She'd grounded me. "Joe can go to the carnival with Imogen," she said. "But you're staying right here. If I find out you've sneaked into town against my orders, you'll forfeit your allowance for a year. And I'm *not even kidding*, Holly."

It was quite a strong threat, I suppose, but nothing, not even financial disaster, was going to keep me from doing my job. Joe had scanned me that morning and sent the results to **POWERS**, who had messaged back a smiley face. I thought that was a bit childish for a governmental agency, but maybe they'd put Mav in charge of the messaging service for the day. Mom had headed off early, giving me yet another lecture before she went. Joe had followed a bit later, one of the walkie-talkies stuffed in his pocket. I had the other, but they had a range of about a half mile, so I'd only be able to contact him when I got into town.

I was on my own in the house, in my suit, and I felt sick.

It wasn't illness. It was the thought that **Macavity** was always there, in the background watching. She'd nearly killed me. She'd nearly killed Imogen, and Joe — and a whole bunch of other innocent people too. She was ruthless and inventive and a genius — and, no one seemed able to catch her.

She wanted to rule the world, she said. And I'd seen what she could do to people with her terrifying technology. She could make people believe anything. She could make them do things they would never do in normal circumstances.

And now she was recruiting. She wanted the invisible twins to work for her. If they said yes, she would have two extremely powerful weapons to manipulate. Because no matter what the twins thought they were getting out of this deal, you could bet that **Macavity** would be getting MORE. She'd be getting two people who could break into anything, anywhere. Two people you'd never suspect, because they were kids.

I'd foiled her plans twice before — and she hated me for it. She would use anything against me. Including invisible superheroes. I had to try to talk to the twins again. I had to try to persuade them to join our side.

I touched the tiny black box at the nape of my neck that was keeping me alive and took a deep breath. It was time to go.

I heard the carnival before I was anywhere near it. Music floated up the hill, and I caught glimpses of brightly-colored flags. The procession would head through the town and along the boardwalk. I figured the twins would be part of the crowd. They'd have tons of opportunities to pick pockets and be a nuisance.

My heart thumped as the crowds thickened. I'd had several curious looks as I'd walked into town, but people had nodded and smiled and assumed I was part of the procession. I'd even seen several people from school, and not one of them had recognized me in my suit. I found myself standing straighter, striding more purposefully. I was **ELECTRIGIRL**! And *no one knew*!

I plunged into the large group of people, looking from left to right, and pulled the walkie-talkie from my belt. "Hey, Joe, I'm here in town."

The walkie-talkie crackled and an irritated voice came out of it. "*Thunderbolt*, remember? Honestly."

"Sorry."

"You're so touchy about your outfit, you'd think you'd understand . . ."

"*Suit*," I said through gritted teeth. "Are you just going to be annoying, or are you going to tell me anything useful?"

"We're by Lucy's Café," Joe said. "Not seen anything weird yet." He raised his voice because a loud brass band was obviously passing. "We'll stay here and let you know if we spot anything."

"OK. Over and out." I slipped the walkie-talkie back onto my belt.

The boardwalk was packed with people, all trying to find a good place along the parade route. Before the floats was a parade of Boy Scouts, Girl Scouts, Navy veterans . . . and the Bluehaven Brass Band, which was presumably what had just reached Joe and Imogen. From the back of the crowd, I could just snatch glimpses of uniforms marching past. The air was full of sugar and spices from the food stands that had been set up along the route. Someone walked past carrying a kebab that smelled so good my mouth watered. As I threaded my way through the crowd, a couple of people commented, "Great costume!" and I smiled at them through gritted teeth. *Suit, it's a suit . . .*

I tripped on a stroller, bumped into a kid, trod on a woman's toe . . . I bet other superheroes didn't spend all their time apologizing!

There was no way I'd be able to spot the invisible twins like this. I could barely see three feet in front of me. What I needed was to get up a bit higher.

Bluehaven's boardwalk has one of those long strings of lights that hang from tall metal posts. You're not supposed to climb them, but . . .

The rubber-soled shoes provided by **POWERS** clung easily to the painted surface, and before I knew it, I was six feet above everyone with an **EXCELLENT** view! I grinned to myself. If only Mr. Blythe, my PE teacher, could see me now!

I stared and stared at the crowds, looking for anything out of the ordinary: a shimmer, a sudden shock — but there was nothing. Just a sea of hundreds and hundreds of people, cheering and clapping as the various groups marched past. Little girls in their rainbow uniforms waved shyly and looked slightly weirded-out. Military men with rows of medals pinned on their uniforms marched solemnly past. The brass band, then a little farther along, a samba band . . .

I looked and looked until my eyes hurt but saw no sign of the invisible thieves. *Patience*, I told myself. *You have a mission. There's still time.*

"Hey, you!" A policewoman was standing at the bottom of my pole, looking up. "I'm sorry, you're not allowed to do that. You'll have to come down."

I hesitated. "I can't," I called back. "Sorry. I'm, um, looking for a friend. This is the only way I can see."

She frowned. "I'm afraid I can't let you stay up there. Didn't you see the signs? No climbing."

Of course I'd seen the signs: I'd seen them every day for years. I shrugged. "Sorry. I'll come down when I find my friend."

"Aren't you supposed to be in the parade?" she called. "In that costume?"

I felt frustrated. What if the invisible twins were passing by me right NOW and she was distracting me from my mission?

MY FINGERS TINGLED . . .

I switched off my powers, silently thanking Dr. Moulford and his little electron stabilizer. Leaving the baffled officer calling after me, I slipped away through the crowd.

IT WAS TIME TO TRY A NEW STRATEGY!

CHAPTER 19

The walking parade was coming to an end: up ahead I could see the slowly looming floats. A large truck decorated as the Wild West glided past, with showgirls in feather boas leaning out and waving cheerfully. Cowboys lounged at the back, chewing on strands of straw. Then there was a float covered entirely in jungle leaves, with children dressed up as tropical birds.

I peered around, ducking and diving, but saw nothing out of the ordinary — no air shimmers, no people being bumped into by invisible people, no giggles . . .

The familiar sound of "Under the Sea" from *The Little Mermaid* reached my ears . . . the preschool float! I slipped to the back of the crowd and waited until my Mom's float had gone past. Standing on tiptoe I could just see the back of it. There was Mom, two small children on her knees, a long blue wig on her head, singing and swaying.

Awww. My mom was a good person.

It was a shame I had to cause her so much trouble.

I turned to face the oncoming floats. Had I been wrong? Were we ALL wrong about the twins being here today?

"Holly," came my brother's voice over the walkie-talkie. "*Holly.*"

"I thought we were supposed to be using code names," I joked back. "All right there, *Thunderbolt?*"

"Holly, this isn't a joke. Holly, *she's here.*"

"Who?" I asked, distracted by something out of the corner of my eye. "Hang on, Joe. I think I just saw something." Sliding the radio back onto my belt, I headed through the crowd. I was sure I'd just seen . . .

Yes! A woman was looking into her handbag. "I'm sure it was here," she said. "I felt a bump."

The twins, it had to be! Carefully, I scanned the crowd. Not there . . . not there . . .

THERE! A slight shimmer to the air, and a man's jacket twitched to one side as he watched the parade.

My powers drained away, as though sucked out of me. A hand clutched my arm as I staggered, and a voice nearby said, "You all right, kid?"

I brushed him off. "I'm fine!" Where was she? How had that eerie voice run through my head — had everyone else heard it too? Where? I turned my head this way and that.

Oh. **OH NO**.

A great gray float was gliding silently along the boardwalk. It played no music; it had no colored flags. It was designed to look like some kind of terrifying prison built on rocks. Walls rose up out of irregularly shaped lumps with square holes cut into them and bars inset. They were prison windows. Little towers with brightly colored cannons perched on the tops. The walls weren't high enough to be life-size; instead, I could see figures behind them, heads peeping over the tops. Children dressed as comedy burglars, just like Sasha had been. Children clutching swag bags — the ones in which old-time burglars would hide their stolen goods. Were they all in on it? Or had Sasha and Dylan realized this was the perfect way to carry out their crimes in plain sight?

And up, up, right at the top of this mountain of gray, was a platform. A single figure stood there in front of a microphone. She was as gray as the hill she stood upon. And her voice hadn't changed at all.

". . . my own profits," she was intoning. "Bluehaven will become a beacon of tourism, of culture, and of wealth."

I felt my teeth press against each other in anger. Because it was all LIES, all of it! I knew her too well. Whatever Macavity was up to, it was for her benefit only!

I brought the walkie-talkie to my mouth in a shaking hand. "Joe," I said, low and urgent. "Joe. Call **POWERS**. Call them NOW. Get them here."

A burble of static was my only response, and I wondered if Joe had even heard me. I stood and stared as the gray monstrosity glided ever nearer.

"To show my gratitude for your faith in me," Macavity said, her monotonous voice drowning out the music being played on the float in front, "I have a present. One lucky person in Bluehaven will find their life changed forever! All you need to do is to press your thumb to the right ticket, and one lucky person will win a hundred thousand dollars!"

Ticket, I thought wildly, what ticket?

"Good luck!" droned **Macavity** — and then, as if on an invisible signal, the child burglars pressed hidden buttons, and thousands of glittery pieces of confetti erupted out of the cannons, showering the crowd.

"Go ahead," said **Macavity**, as the float slid silently on its way. "Press your thumb to any ticket you find. The winning ticket will light up instantly and you will have won a hundred thousand dollars!"

Chaos broke out. The crowd surged forward, reaching for the glittery confetti. Children were knocked over; adults clashed heads as they jumped for the tickets. Excited screaming filled the air as people pushed and shoved their way to grabbing as many tickets as possible, pressing their thumbs to the paper in eagerness, and then discarding them immediately when the ticket didn't light up.

I was bumped and jostled as people rushed past me. I couldn't move. What could I do? **Macavity** had turned the whole town crazy!

CHAPTER 20

The air was full of fluttering tickets. The gray float was gliding off down the boardwalk, Macavity's voice booming as it went. And as the crowds up ahead caught on, they too went bonkers, climbing over each other to snatch the shimmering tickets. People screamed, children cried, and I overheard someone nearby say, "That Macavity is the best thing to have happened to Bluehaven in a long time."

Fury filled me. Had they all forgotten what she'd done with her evil cell phones? Did they have no understanding of what was happening right now, right at this very moment? Could they not see the *danger* Macavity was putting people in, as they trampled one another in their greed for money?

I didn't care what she was really up to. I just had to stop her. It was time to get moving.

I shoved my way through the angry mass of bodies in front and toppled forward into the road, behind the prison float. I gritted my teeth at the stinging from my knee and scrambled to my feet. The float was about seventy feet ahead now, and the one behind it had been forced to come to a complete halt because of the people scrambling around on the ground for tickets. I swung around wildly, trying to take in the full picture, wondering what on earth I could do.

If I could stop the prison float, then at least the damage would be limited to this area only. The golden tickets had only just been released; stopping the float here would prevent chaos along the whole length of the boardwalk.

I ran after the float, jumping over people who were on all-fours and trying not to trip over bags and strollers left lying in the street.

AS I RAN, I SWITCHED ON MY POWERS . . .

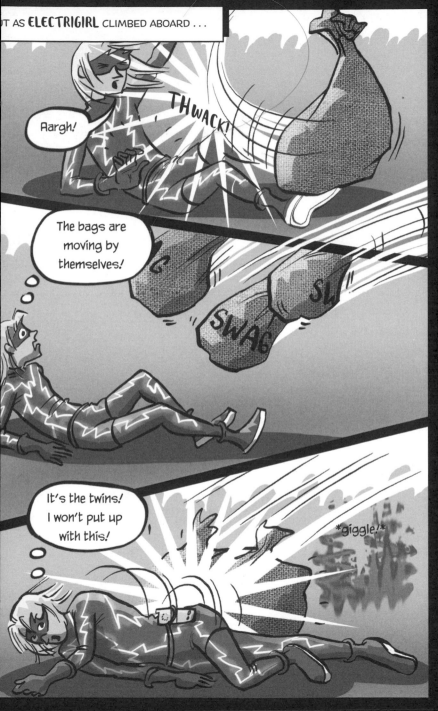

CHAPTER 21

You know that moment when you wake up before you open your eyes? When everything is still dark, but you become aware of your senses?

Well, everything *really* ached. "Ow," I thought. My legs felt as though they had run a marathon. My arms lay heavy, as though I'd lifted a building. My head . . .

Wait.

I wasn't dead.

WHOA!

I WASN'T DEAD!

With shaking fingers, I felt for the back of my neck. There, firmly stuck and definitely not cracked or broken, was a new electron stabilizer.

I opened my eyes, stiffly. I don't know what I was expecting to see, but it wasn't this.

I was in my own bedroom. Tucked into the covers on my bed, like a child, in my pajamas.

What time was it? How did I get here? I struggled to remember. I was on the parade float, reaching up for **Macavity's** legs . . .

My eyes jerked open wide. **Macavity!** Had she escaped? What had happened?

I was sitting up before I'd even decided to do it, and actually it was the wrong decision because I fell off the bed.

Good thing no one was there to see me do th— oh.

"You're awake," said my brother from the doorway.

I waved at him from the floor, trying to pretend I had totally meant to do that. "Hi. I, uh, I just thought the floor looked comfy."

Joe grinned. "Yeah, right. Here." He hauled me up and helped me sink back onto the bed. "Steve said you might be kind of woozy for a while."

"He did? He was here? How did *I* get here?"

"**POWERS** got us all back here before Mom. She didn't even know you'd left the house. She thinks you've been sleeping off your guilt over the costume shop fire."

Imogen appeared in the doorway too, grinning at me. "Hi, Holly. Well done."

"Well done?" I rubbed my head. "I did the right thing? So . . . what *did* I do?"

Imogen came in, closing the door behind her. "You . . . well, you sort of went bang. You know. With the electricity thing."

Joe rolled his eyes. "It was an electromagnetic pulse," he told me. "You took out all the electrical equipment within a half-mile radius. Including **Macavity's** helicopter."

"What happened?" I demanded. "Did it land on people? Did I hurt anyone?"

"Chill." Imogen put a hand on my arm. "It fell in the sea. Like a big stone. The pilot managed to get out before the cabin filled up with water and ended up sitting on top of it, waiting to be rescued." She started to laugh. "And **Macavity** was bobbing in the waves, screaming about how she couldn't swim . . . and then she realized it was only about waist deep where she was."

"People waded in to help her," Joe said, also chuckling. "And you could tell she really wanted to get away, but everyone was offering her cups of tea and blankets and saying she should go to the hospital. It was really funny."

I smiled. "I bet she hated that! But I guess . . . well, she got away with it again, didn't she?"

Joe shook his head. "We haven't gotten to the best part. **POWERS** turned up in all their black trucks again, except they couldn't get near the boardwalk because of all the people and vehicles that couldn't move. Oh — you shut down the engines of all the cars and trucks, Holly. It was pretty impressive, but the whole place is taped off because they have to tow everything away."

"Oh dear," I said.

"Another expensive tidy-up job for **POWERS**," agreed Imogen. "But I don't think they mind. Not this time."

I stared from one to the other of them. "What is it? Spit it out!"

"**Macavity's** behind bars," burst out Imogen. Her smile was so wide you could mail a letter through it.

"What?"

Joe nodded. "Yup. Would you believe one of the lawyers she hired did something illegal?"

"How very surprising," I said sarcastically.

"And when he was taken in for questioning, he spilled everything, including **Macavity's** misuse of public funds, or something."

"But . . .," I said, confused, "that's not . . . I mean . . . what about all her other crimes?"

Joe shrugged. "Steve said they didn't know if they could ever make them stick. You need something that you can prove — and she's so good at leaving no traces."

"What about the DNA she was collecting?" I asked, the memories flooding back. "There was a computer in the float."

The other two stared at me. "What?"

"You must know about it!" I cried. "Those golden confetti tickets — you know, the ones you had to press your thumb against to see if you were going to win the money. They were transmitting people's DNA back to a computer in the float! Didn't **POWERS** find it when they looked through everything?"

Joe and Imogen looked at each other. "There might well have been a computer . . .," said Imogen slowly, "but Holly . . . you broke everything. Including computers."

The truth sunk in. "So there is no evidence there . . .," I said, sinking back into the bed. "I destroyed the evidence against her — *again*."

"But hey," Imogen said, trying to sound cheerful, "she's locked up. **POWERS** have got her. And they won't be letting her out if they can help it."

I nodded, feeling a bit better. "That's true. An all-around win for **POWERS** then, what with the invisible twins too."

"Oh. Well . . ." Imogen and Joe both went pink.

I frowned. "They have the twins too, right? You were sitting on them!"

"Well, we were," said Imogen. "But we sort of . . . had to get up."

"It wasn't our fault," said Joe defensively. "This police officers came along and accused us of pickpocketing. All this stuff fell out of one of the swag bags — cell phones and watches and stuff — and he thought we were responsible. He thought we were mocking them, sitting on thin air. He got really mad and made us get up. It took a long time to explain we had nothing to do with the stolen items."

"And the twins got away," admitted Imogen. "Sorry."

"But school starts again next week," said Joe. "So I'll be able to keep an eye on them then. Maybe I could try talking to them. I might have better luck than you did."

"Yeah, yeah, all right," I said. "So overall, we did OK. We've lost the twins, but **Macavity** is behind bars. And I made everything electrical stop working … oh, does that include cash registers and cell phones, and TVs and ovens in people's houses, and street lights and … ?" I stopped, because the others were nodding. "Oh. That's … expensive."

"But it wasn't the electricity in the whole country," pointed out Imogen. "And hey, you're not dead!"

"Yeah," said Joe. "Thanks for not exploding." He shrugged in a careless way.

Suddenly I hugged him. "Hey! What're you doing?" He threw me off. "Weirdo."

I laughed. "No word from **POWERS** then? No scanning you want to do on your priceless Gadget?"

He gave me a look.

"What?"

"Holly, you are SO dense sometimes. The Gadget's electronic. You busted it."

"Oh! Oh Joe, I'm so sorry."

"It's all right. Steve said they'll give me a new one." He sighed. "But in the meantime, we've got to go back to the old pager." He pulled it out of his pocket. "Remember this? A two-line screen! Text only! It's like we're back in the Dark Ages when you first got your powers!"

"Hand it over," said Imogen.

Joe tossed it to her — and the pager fell onto the floor. "Butterfingers," he said.

Imogen frowned and bent to pick it up — and her fingers seemed to pass right through the pager. "What the . . . ?" She tried again — and again, her fingers were unable to grip it, as if they weren't solid.

"Imogen," I said quietly. "What's the matter with your hand?"

She held it up in front of her face. It looked solid enough. "I don't . . . it feels . . . *normal* . . ."

Joe reached forward with his own hand . . . and it passed through Imogen's.

Joe pulled it back with a jerk. "*Whoa!*" Then he reached for Imogen's other hand, which clasped his firmly. "It's just the one hand," he said.

"You have a . . . ghost hand," I said in amazement. "Whoa."

She stared at me, eyes wide. "It must be the green goo."

"The Diabola," I said. "That's what she called it. But why . . . how can we still see your hand? Why isn't it invisible like the twins?"

"Holly, what am I going to *do*?" Imogen cried.

"Relax," I said. "We just need to call Steve. **POWERS** sorted out my power problem, didn't they?" I tapped the back of my neck. "I'm sure they can fix your ghostly hand too."

"It might be quite *useful* to have a ghostly hand . . .," considered Joe. "Just think — you could unlock doors from the other side, by passing your hand right through the wood!"

"*No*," said Imogen firmly. "I want it fixed. One superhuman is quite enough for Bluehaven! And it's my right hand . . . How am I going to, you know . . .," she lowered her voice to a whisper, "*wipe my bottom?*"

Joe burst into laughter.

"You have *another* hand, Imogen," I told her, trying not to smile. "Listen, **Macavity's** behind bars, and I'm not dead. If a ghostly hand is our only worry, I think we're doing OK."

"You've forgotten one thing," Joe said. "One really, really awful thing."

Imogen and I stared at him. "What?"

He took a deep breath. "*School* starts next week."

I thought about it. Homework, teachers, Scarlett May the school bully . . . Then I grinned. "You know what?" I said . . .

WHICH ELECTRIGIRL CHARACTER ARE YOU?

1. IT'S A SUNNY SUMMER DAY! WOULD YOU RATHER SPEND IT:

   A running up a giant hill, rolling down it, and repeating until you get dizzy

   B eating ice cream on the beach while reading your favorite superhero comic

   C painting a picture of the way the light catches the water on the sea

   D drinking coffee and scrolling through gadget websites on your phone

2. WHAT DRIVES YOU CRAZY THE MOST?

   A having to sit still for an hour

   B people who don't know the difference between Marvel and DC

   C being interrupted when you're in the middle of a craft project

   D people who don't know how to operate their own TV remote

3. WHERE WOULD YOU GO ON VACATION?

   A a road trip across the USA — all those open skies and all that space to run around in!

   B Gotham City. If not that, a film set, or somewhere you could meet Stan Lee

C The Palace of Versailles, because it has amazing chandeliers and a hall of mirrors!

D a world tour of all the locations used in the James Bond films

4. WHAT MAKES A GOOD FRIEND?

A someone who's always there for you, even when you're not fully in control of your feelings

B someone who can hold the camera for you and knows they'll always be Robin to your Batman

C someone who lets you be yourself and doesn't mind that you want to be alone sometimes

D someone who dresses in black a lot and knows what NSA stands for

5. IN AN IDEAL WORLD . . .

A everyone would do all their classes outside because it's not good to be cooped up inside

B people would think for themselves, not blindly follow others

C more people would understand how important the creative arts are to happiness

D you would be James Bond

RESULTS...

Mostly As: You are Holly! You're energetic and you hate boring routines. Go out there and save the world! Just make sure you listen to the people around you and try not to make decisions before you know all the facts!

Mostly Bs: You are Joe! You wish the world were more like it is in comics, with good always triumphing over evil. Your belief in the power of good is really important. But don't forget that there may be other cool things in the world that might not actually be superhero-related!

Mostly Cs: You are Imogen! You like to be quiet and to take in everything around you, and you find painting and art to be relaxing. Make sure you take time for yourself because other people can be tiring. But don't forget to have fun too!

Mostly Ds: You are Maverick! Always with one eye on the future and a keen nose for danger, you like to live life on the edge. Slow down and appreciate the here and now! You could be missing something good by thinking too far ahead!

ABOUT THE AUTHOR

Jo Cotterill believes that superheroes are really important. They are what we can all aspire to be: people who use their powers to fight evil and help others. When she's not trying to change the world, Jo makes up stories in her very untidy office-slah-craft room, sometimes stopping to write music instead. Her other books include the Sweet Hearts series for Random House and the critically-acclaimed *Looking at the Stars*, which was nominated for the Carnegie Medal. Jo lives in Oxfordshire, England, with her husband, daughters, and two overindulged guinea pigs.

jocotterill.com

ABOUT THE ILLUSTRATOR

Cathy Brett has been a theater scenic artist, school art technician, college lecturer, fashion illustrator, packaging designer, jet-setting spotter of global trends, and style consultant to the British high street. These days she loves drawing more than anything else. Ever. Except her nieces. And cake. Drawing her nieces while eating cake would be utter bliss.

Cathy lives and works in a shed-slash-studio at the bottom of a Surrey, England, garden.

cathybrett.blogspot.co.uk

DESIGN A SUPERSUIT

Use this superhero template to create your own supersuit. Trace the outline onto a piece of paper, draw your design over the top, and give your new superhero a name!

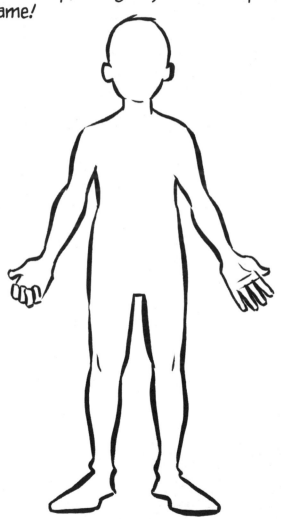